FRÉDÉRIC DARD

THE KING OF FOOLS

TRANSLATED BY LOUISE ROGERS LALAURIE

First published in French as *La Pelouse* in 1952

First published by Pushkin Vertigo in 2017

This book is supported by the Institut français
(Royaume-Uni) as part of the Burgess Programme

1 3 5 7 9 8 6 4 2

ISBN: 9781782271970

Text designed and typeset by Tetragon, London
Printed and bound by CPI Group (UK) Ltd, Croydon CRO 4YY

www.pushkinpress.com

Whose dark or troubled mind will you step into next? Detective or assassin, victim or accomplice? How can you tell reality from delusion when you're spinning in the whirl of a thriller, or trapped in the grip of an unsolvable mystery? When you can't trust your senses, or anyone you meet; that's when you know you're in the hands of the undisputed masters of crime fiction.

Writers of the greatest thrillers and mysteries on earth, who inspired those that followed. Their books are found on shelves all across their home countries—from Asia to Europe, and everywhere in between. Timeless tales that have been devoured, adored and handed down through the decades. Iconic books that have inspired films, and demand to be read and read again. And now we've introduced Pushkin Vertigo Originals—the greatest contemporary crime writing from across the globe, by some of today's best authors.

So step inside a dizzying world of criminal masterminds with **Pushkin Vertigo**. The only trouble you might have is leaving them behind.

1

When I saw her climb into my car, I thought she was planning to steal it, and hurried out of the restaurant, still clutching my napkin. Outside, in the harsh midday sun, I found her settled in the passenger seat, leafing through a tourist guide. She was small, with a ruddy complexion and colourless hair matted with seawater. She wore a green towelling beach robe, and the water trickled down her neck, losing itself in the opening of her bathing suit. The sudden cast of my shadow across the pages of her book caught her attention. She raised her eyes and gazed thoughtfully at me, trying to discover what this fellow in swimming shorts, idiotically twisting his red-and-white chequered napkin, could possibly want from her. Curiously, it was I who felt awkward. We stared at one another in this way for some time. She seemed perfectly at ease, like a person with right on their side.

"I'm so sorry," I stammered, at length. "You're... you're in my car."

She had thick eyebrows which she obviously never plucked; they gave a depth to her pale eyes. The eyebrows were frowning in surprise now.

"I don't understand – your car?" she said quietly.

She was English, and spoke French with an almost comically English accent. Her small, girlish voice didn't suit her at all. It put me in mind of the shrill, silly tones of the sheriff's daughter in a badly dubbed Western. It irritated me.

"You're sitting in my car," I ventured, glumly. "Not that I have a particularly acute sense of private property, but I should like to know why."

She listened attentively, her lips silently forming one or two words whose meaning was unclear. The effect was rather like an operatic diva singing her partner's words in her head during a grand duet. She shut her book and stared around her in astonishment, then promptly burst out laughing and pointed to a white MG parked in front of my vehicle, and identical to mine in all points. It bore a British number plate.

"Oh, I'm terribly sorry!" she breathed, opening the passenger door.

It was my turn to laugh, at her embarrassment. This was just the sort of mistake a person was likely to make in the bustle of Juan-les-Pins in August, coming up from the beach with sand, salt and sun in their eyes.

"It's the same, isn't it?" she said, pointing to the other MG.

"They might be twins," I agreed.

"Yours has red upholstery too."

"Yes. But your steering wheel's on the right!"

Her expression darkened, as if my remark had annoyed her.

"How stupid. I don't understand..."

"What don't you understand?"

"How I could have made such a mistake."

And then, suddenly, she was very British once again. She realized she was talking to a man to whom she hadn't been introduced, and left me standing outside the restaurant, with its wooden deck that smelt like a floating lido. I returned to my meal, trying hard not to glance outside. When I emerged, the Englishwoman's MG had disappeared.

I settled myself behind the wheel of my car and drove to my hotel, a short distance out of town. Each day after lunch I took a siesta in my room, since it was impossible to sleep at night: an open-air nightclub raged just twenty metres away. Jumping out of my open-topped car, I spotted her beach bag lying forgotten under the dashboard, unnoticed by me until now because it was black, like the carpet covering the floor of the MG. It contained an English novel, a bottle of suntan oil, sunglasses, a towel and a tiny soft toy – a lion. The gold plastic glasses case contained a thousand francs. The forgotten bag worried me. I had no desire to go looking for the ruddy-faced girl to give it back. I took the bag and tossed it into the empty half of my wardrobe.

The air in my room was mild, even cool. The closed shutters kept the room dark and filtered the sluggish afternoon sounds, though they were useless at night against the din from the "Makao". I stretched out naked on my bed. I crossed my arms behind my head and drifted into a daydream. At this time of day I was clear-headed and at peace. It was the mornings that depressed me more than anything, after a few hours of poor sleep. Then, life seemed empty and I hated this holiday.

I should have been with Denise, but we had broken off just two days before leaving, on some petty pretext. For a moment, I had considered cancelling my trip, but then decided the Côte d'Azur would be a timely distraction, and left anyway. I regretted it now. Holiday resorts are best approached in a happy frame of mind, or they can seem more depressing than all the rest. Truth be told, my sorrow was not acute. Rather, I experienced a feeling of intense disenchantment that left me weak and vulnerable.

I felt the nagging torment of physical regret too. With Denise, the act of love had been easy, and reassuring. At length I fell asleep, as I had every other day. And like every other day, I woke again around four o'clock in the afternoon. I closed the shutter slats tightly against the relentless sun. The sounds from outside took on a different quality now. The gravelly voice of the sea rose above the racket of Juan-les-Pins.

I forgot all about the Englishwoman of that morning.

In the evening, when not tempted by a show, I would spend an hour or two at the casino. I'm not a gambler, but I enjoy the atmosphere in the gaming halls. I find their tense, solemn mood exhilarating; I'm touched by the pale, serious faces under the light of the table lamps, clinging hard to their mask of composure. If Hell is staffed with attendants, they are surely recruited from the deceased croupiers of this world. Their unruffled insouciance is in such contrast to the punters' veneer of fake calm that they seem truly demonic. I never sat at the card tables, because I played little, and with none of the systems and strategies that most players insist on following. I preferred roulette, placing a straight-up bet two or three times in a row. Each time, I would concentrate like an athlete before attempting some feat of prowess. I would think hard about a number until it came to seem so obvious, so utterly natural, that a moment later I was astonished to see the ball drop into a different pocket. I felt that Luck herself had made a mistake, or humiliated me quite deliberately.

That evening, I remember playing the 5, then the 14, and then the 5 once again. Within minutes, I was fifteen thousand francs down. Par for the course. And so I played one last time, but differently: I placed fifteen thousand francs on red. If the ball dropped into a black pocket, I would be thirty thousand francs down. But if the number was red, I would recoup my losses and leave. A true player would smile at my low-roller methods; and indeed, I caught a few ironic glances from one or two regulars who had been following my stakes. I didn't care. I'm the son of provincial shopkeepers, and my parents taught me one thing above all: the value of money.

Slightly shame-faced, I placed three five-thousand-franc chips on red.

As I withdrew my hand, I saw a ravishing young woman smiling at me from across the table. She held a small pile of chips in her left hand. She counted fifteen thousand francs and placed them on black, her eyes fixed upon mine all the while. I was astonished; her gesture was clearly a challenge. I wondered where I had seen her before. The croupier spun the wheel and tossed the ball with a small, practised flick of the wrist.

I kept my eyes fixed on the young woman, wondering where and how we had met. A long time ago, it seemed to me. I searched her features for a different face, like someone determined to rediscover the child's visage in that of an adult.

The ball landed on red. The girl pursed her lips in disappointment, and in that small expression of frustration I recognized her. My Englishwoman of that morning. I was spellbound. How could the ruddy-faced girl in the MG have transformed into this elegant, attractive young creature? I rounded the table.

"What a delightful surprise!"

"You've forgotten your winnings," she whispered, indicating the expanse of green baize.

I shrugged carelessly.

"Play again," I said quietly, struggling to affect the light tones of a man for whom a fifteen-thousand-franc stake is a mere trifle.

"I was wrong to try and play against you!"

She wore her hair in a swept-up style that enhanced its warm chestnut colour and reddish tints, held in place on top of her head by a narrow gold clip decorated with closely spaced links like the scales of a fish. Her complexion had looked ruddy that morning, but in reality it was just a touch of sunburn – a natural foundation that offset her understated make-up to astonishing effect. She wore a green dress, not too low-cut, with a black lace rose pinned to her chest. Not exactly the last word in Parisian chic, but it suited her well.

I heard the clicking of the ball on the mahogany track. This time, the number was black, swallowing my thirty thousand francs. I seized the moment to escort my companion to the bar.

"Champagne?"

She laughed.

"Of course! We impoverished English never miss the chance of a glass of bubbly."

"You know you forgot your beach bag in my car?"

"Yes. I was annoyed about the sunglasses, but I hoped I would see you again…"

She hoped she'd see me again, to retrieve her sunglasses. But the way she said it did me the power of good. I couldn't take my eyes off her. She was charming, graceful, with a gentle beauty I had never seen in a woman before.

"Why are you staring at me like that?" she asked, eventually. "Is something the matter?"

"Yes. You're very beautiful."

She glanced away, then after a brief pause, she spoke again.

"The first time I came to France was on an organized tour, when I was a little girl. Before we left, the guide gave us heaps of advice. Among other things, he said that the first thing a Frenchman will do once he's alone with a woman is to tell her she's beautiful."

"So glad I didn't disappoint, *Mademoiselle*."

"*Madame!*"

"Oh! I'm so sorry. And I still haven't introduced myself: Jean-Marie Valaise."

"My name is Faulks. Marjorie Faulks."

The waiter brought our champagne and prepared to pour. But I told him to let the bottle chill. I wanted to prolong our tête-à-tête.

"I said you were beautiful precisely because this morning you seemed quite the opposite," I declared, coldly.

She nodded.

"This morning you took me for a thief, and worse still, I had just come up from the beach, red as a lobster. But I think you're mistaken now. I'm not pretty."

I stared at her, unabashed, as if contemplating a portrait. Was she pretty? Perhaps not, indeed. She had an Englishwoman's mouth, with a receding lower jaw. She traced her upper lip with her fingernail. She must have been reading my thoughts.

"And *then* there are my freckles," she sighed.

"*Des bulles de champagne!*"

"*Des*… what?"

"Champagne bubbles – perhaps you don't know the word?"

"No."

I showed her the bottle of Pommery.

"Look, there."

Her face took on a delighted expression, and she repeated the word *bulles* wonderingly, several times over, watching the champagne sparkle. Except she pronounced it "bool", and my best efforts to teach the proper elocution produced nothing but a comical "bee-yool". I noticed with surprise that her voice was fuller and deeper than this morning.

We drank a first glass of champagne. Marjorie savoured her drink with eyes closed. Suddenly, it occurred to me that she had not come to the Côte d'Azur alone. She had climbed into the passenger seat of my car, and seemed to be waiting for someone. The thought was vaguely annoying.

"Are you staying at a hotel?"

"No, I'm with some friends from home. They've rented a villa in Cap d'Antibes."

"Are you here for long?"

"I'm flying back tomorrow evening."

I felt an almost physical pang of disappointment. I was the boyish flirt, rubbing his neighbour's foot at dinner, delighted to discover she wasn't moving it away, only to find it was the table leg all along.

"What a shame."

The champagne tasted warm, and too young.

"Yes, it is a shame. I love it here on the Côte d'Azur. English people always… Well, it was we who discovered it, after all!"

"Indeed. It was a British colony for years. Are you travelling with your husband?"

"No, he hasn't been able to take any holiday yet, this year. Too much work. He's an architect. He's building a big school on the outskirts of London at the moment. And what do you do?"

"A great deal of travelling!" I replied. "I sell office adding machines for an American firm."

"And how many do you sell?"

"I couldn't say exactly, I'd need an adding machine…"

We chatted for almost an hour, against the murmur of the casino. Pale plumes of smoke curled around the lamps, and our eyes drooped. Marjorie pulled herself up so suddenly that it took me a moment to realize she was leaving.

"I'm meeting my friends, and I'm terribly late. Thank you for the champagne…"

"Your beach bag!" I stammered, startled by her sudden departure.

"Which is your hotel?"

"The Palmier Bleu. It's—"

"I'll send someone for it! Goodbye!"

She disappeared into the crowd. I would have chased after her, but I had to pay for the champagne, and the barman was busy.

2

That evening, I drank a little in hopes of knocking myself out. But all I got was a vile headache.

I went back to my hotel. I had a raging thirst. I drank stale water from the tap, but was unable to quench it. Like the water, my life bore the taint of rust in the pipe work. The Makao's neon sign flashed through the slats in the shutters. Watched for too long, it could make a man want to scream. I fell asleep around 4 a.m., as every night. When I woke, my headache was no better. Miserably, I dragged myself under the shower. I felt better for the thousand needles gushing from the rose. I switched between hot and cold, hunching my back and offering my stiff neck to the fierce downpour.

A decent coffee and an aspirin restored my spirits. I would go and laze on the beach, and life would start up again, like the dough hook on a kitchen mixer. I would be swept into the daily round. What else could I hope for? Holidays, the sun, the casino, the fish soup suppers? And then Paris, and Denise's telephone call! And my clients, to whom I would demonstrate the wonders of the ACT adding machine. I wasn't a family man, but I had my routine. I shivered in my robe, my teeth chattering, and decided to go back to bed for five minutes, to warm up. When I stepped back into my room, Marjorie was there, sitting demurely with both hands clasped over one knee. She wore white shorts and a striped sailor shirt. Her face was scrubbed and her hair was tied back with a ribbon. She looked delighted at my horrified expression.

"I know it's not the done thing, but the Côte d'Azur is the sort of place where a person feels like doing something they shouldn't."

I felt awkward and clumsy in my robe, with water trickling down my hair and legs. I could find nothing to say. I couldn't offer her a seat because she was already sitting down.

"I came to fetch the bag myself. I rushed off rather too suddenly last night… I did knock. But with the noise from the shower… Don't you lock your door?"

"Not in a hotel."

"Why ever not?"

"So that people like you can walk in, I expect."

In place of a smile, her face darkened, as if she were deeply offended. She seemed about to leave. But she stayed. Her pale eyes wandered to the open window. The view was unexpected for such a sought-after resort: electricity pylons, apartment blocks, a garage.

A mechanic in blue overalls was washing an old car that was hardly worth the effort. The jet whistled against the bodywork. I walked over to the wardrobe, opened it and took out the beach bag.

"Here are your things."

She sat the bag on her knees. For reasons unknown, she looked sulky and frightened all at once. Like a little girl who has been ticked off in public and is trying not to cry.

"It's very kind of you to come, Mrs Faulks."

"Call me Marjorie."

"Thank you, I've been dying to. It's such a pretty name. To me, Marjorie is like *Ma Jolie* in French."

The room had only one chair, so I sat on the edge of the bed, taking care to fold the flaps of my robe over my hairy legs.

Now she was looking at the photograph of Denise on my bedside table. The picture stood in a small leather frame, a gift from Denise herself, who had made me promise to take it everywhere I went.

"Is that your sister?"

"No, the very idea!"

"She looks like you."

"By some kind of osmosis, then. I spent six years of my life with that woman."

"And now?"

"Now it's over, *provisoirement*."

She was interested, and watched me intently, anxious to catch every word.

"What does that mean, *provisoirement*?"

"It means that once or twice a year we say our goodbyes, but get back together again three weeks later. One of us calls the other and we carry on."

"Is that love?"

"Of a kind."

"One day you won't call."

"I know. Perhaps that day has come."

"She's pretty."

"Much more than in that picture."

"She's got plenty of character. Sharp eyes."

"Yes, plenty."

"Do you live together?"

"No, that's how we keep going."

"What does she do?"

"She has a little couture house near the Champs-Elysées. Practically the size of this room. She never has more than three or four dresses for sale, but those three or four are like nothing you've ever seen."

Now she knew more about Denise than she did about me. Oddly, Denise formed a kind of bond between us. The patron saint of our relationship.

"Are you still leaving tonight?"

"Yes. My husband's expecting me."

"What's he like?"

"Serious type. Tall and thin, with a prominent Adam's apple."

"Any children?"

"No."

We had nothing more to say. She stood up and flattened the front of her shorts in that way all women do. She hooked the string of her black bag over one finger and swung it gently back and forth. From time to time, it knocked against her lovely, tanned legs with a soft thud. I can tell an unhappy person, especially one who tries to keep it hidden. I sensed she was burdened with a sorrow she was struggling to conceal. But sorrow is like rust: it will surface, however thick the layer of paint we apply to cover it up.

"Well, er, I'll be going then…"

It was an infinitely fragile moment. A word, a gesture, even a look, and it would be gone.

"Delighted to have met you, *Monsieur* Valaise."

We shook hands and she left. I should have seen her to the door but I stayed sitting on the bed, my head lowered, sunk in an ill-defined feeling of anguish. Every woman has her own aura. Marjorie's manifested itself above all when she left a room. Her aura remained, stronger and more troubling than her presence. I stared at the pink and green chintz-covered chair. I felt a terrible sense of having lost something beautiful. Just a few seconds before, anything had been possible. The merest hint. A hint that she – or I – could have acted on. But she hadn't dared. And neither had I. A faint light had glimmered between us, and now it had gone out.

Shyly, the door reopened. She stood framed in the doorway, not daring to step over the threshold. A short time ago she had marched straight into my room, like a conquered territory, and now she was afraid to come back in. I saw she was holding something out to me. The little toy lion from her beach bag.

"Take this," she stammered, "if you like?"

I moved towards the door. But it was her wrist I took hold of, leading her into the room. I pushed the door shut with my elbow and took Marjorie in my arms. She gave no sign of resistance, no tremor of excitement. She was passive, like a drowned person pulled along in the current. And the strangest thing of all was that I actually compared her to a drowned woman, there and then. Heavy in my arms, docile to the point of inertia, she leaned her weight against mine, burying her face in the opening of my bathrobe, stock-still. After a while, I lifted her head gently and saw she was crying.

"Tell me what's wrong, Marjorie."

She recovered herself as quickly as she had let go. She hardened her features, and dried her eyes in a blink.

"I'm sorry. So stupid of me."

She pressed the toy lion into my hand.

"I call him Pug," she said, "because he looks like a dog I had when I was little. I hope he brings you good luck. Take good care of him!" she added, with an embarrassed smile.

Pug was a cheap fairground trinket, but I could see Marjorie was making a sacrifice.

The tiny lion had a debonair expression and his mane looked a little like Fidel Castro's beard; grains of white sand escaped from a small slit in his side.

"I will," I promised.

This rather ridiculous scene reminded me of a film that had made a great impression on me as a child. It was the story of an aviator who goes to war with a small teddy bear around his neck, given to him by his young wife. One day, he leaves the bear behind in his room and, naturally, is shot down in flames during a dog fight. The film ended with a close-up of the abandoned bear lying on top of a trunk. I cried myself to sleep for days after, thinking about the little lost animal, the symbol – in my eyes – of every lost love, every thwarted destiny, the misery of the whole world.

"May I write to you, Marjorie?"

My question seemed to surprise her.

And then her face lit up and she answered in a smiling, lilting voice, "Oh! Yes!"

"Thank you. I just need your address."

Her face darkened for a moment.

"My address – that's impossible. Send your letter poste restante to the London GPO."

"I will."

"I don't want to force you. Promise me you'll only write if you really want to!"

"I promise."

Seconds before, I might have kissed her, perhaps even taken her to my bed. But now once more we were a man and woman who barely knew one another, and we parted on a handshake.

3

She could scarcely have turned the corner of the street before I began my letter.

> My dear Marjorie,
>
> When I first saw you in my car, I should have got behind the wheel before you had time to get out, and driven off like a madman…

I wrote six pages that I felt like tossing into the waste paper basket, for I was certain they could never express or even come close to reflecting my state of mind.

There are people we get to know gradually in life, and then there are others we meet and recognize straight away. Such people stay in our hearts for ever. I had "recognized" Marjorie. Since leaving the room, her memory was stronger with every passing minute. I had spent six years with Denise, and our relationship had brought nothing. After less than an hour with Mrs Faulks, I was a richer man. I refrained from reading my letter back, knowing that if I did, I would never post it.

It was an odd day: neither happy nor sad. White, like the sky. By tossing my letter into the post box, I set the mechanism in motion, and could decide nothing until it had run its course.

I lazed at the beach, indifferent to the other bathers, or the extraordinary green sea shimmering on the horizon. I took no lunch, nor an afternoon siesta. Curled in my parasol's dark circle of shade, I wriggled bad-temperedly in the sand, following its orbit.

I told myself that Marjorie was still in Juan-les-Pins, until that evening. I could have searched for her in the happy crowds, but I had no desire to try. I would have to wait a while before risking a reunion. I needed to wait for her! When I reached my hotel at the end of the afternoon I was hungry and tired from lying for so long on the beach, doing nothing. The proprietor was bringing in a basket of lobsters. He called out to me.

"Monsieur Valaise! Did you see the lady waiting for you on the terrace?"

I felt a flash of heat at the back of my skull.

"A lady," I muttered, staring at the lobsters awkwardly waving their antennae.

The hotel owner was a large, pleasant man, invariably clad in a short-sleeved blue shirt and linen trousers, both lacking their share of buttons. He winked.

"Not a bad-looking lady."

Marjorie! I dashed through the lobby. Beyond, there was a terrace of sorts where the hotel residents would take a last drink before bed. A green-tiled water feature added an exotic touch, decorated with tubs of banana trees and a palm with bark like the hide of an elephant.

Denise was sitting in a swing seat, its chains mewing under her weight. My disappointment was so strong it crashed over me like a wave of nausea.

Wearily, I approached the swing seat. Denise wore a white silk two-piece suit. She had taken off her shoes and folded her legs under her. The dainty pumps, woven with threads of gold, looked out of place on the patio tiles.

"Try not to look so pleased," she declared, with a hearty, sad laugh.

She was beautiful, enticing. Around her floated the discreet scent of Parisian elegance. She was Paris itself.

"I wasn't expecting you to visit," I muttered, delivering a lukewarm kiss.

"To visit! Hark at you! Since when do we pay visits to one another, you and I?"

She caressed my cheek and her touch was full of tenderness.

"So you've found a replacement?"

"Don't be silly!"

She stared into the depths of my soul, then nodded like a doctor reserving her final diagnosis.

"I decided on the spur of the moment," she said with a sigh, stroking her velvet hand against my sand-pocked face. "I still wasn't sure whether to come this morning. Then it struck me at lunchtime, on the Champs-Elysées, looking at a travel agent's window. Posters have a strangely evocative power, don't they? I went in and asked if there was a plane to Nice this afternoon. There was. Do you still love me?"

"*Je t'aime.*"

"How's it been without me?"

"It's been."

"Good or bad? Do try and be a little charming, at least? Tell me some lies."

"It's been all right. Grey, mild, dull, neutral, it's been..."

"OK, OK. Me too. Any conquests?"

"None."

Marjorie's face loomed in my mind with extraordinary force, then slowly broke apart. The effect was like a slip of the hand, when you reach out to place the last piece in a jigsaw puzzle.

"You surely wouldn't have me believe you're a holiday virgin?"

"I may not have you believe it, but it's true all the same."

She stood up and searched for her shoes with her feet, across the tiles. A fat green-and-blue dragonfly hovered around a banana leaf like a tiny helicopter in distress.

"Your hotel's not bad, but the neighbourhood looks rather like back home in Asnières, don't you think?"

"I prefer Asnières," I assured her.

She burst out laughing. She was standing in her shoes now, holding out her hand to me with an inviting look.

"Are you coming?"

Her cases were in the hall, near the coat stand. The owner had been watching and came over as I bent to grasp the handles.

"Leave those, Monsieur Valaise, I'll bring them up."

"No need!"

We were already on the stairs when he asked, with a barely suppressed smirk, "Two breakfasts for tomorrow?"

"That's right, two!"

4

I woke next morning feeling in tune with the whole world. I was happy and relaxed. Why this comforting sense of having escaped some form of danger? I felt like a man recovering from a bout of illness.

I rose, feeling wonderfully light on my feet. The sun poured through the chinks in the shutters, streaking the room with gold. I walked over to the window and propped the slats half open. The garage mechanic opposite was polishing a little red sports car. It looked like a toy, and gazing at it, by a process of association, I thought of Marjorie Faulks. I had forgotten all about her until that moment. She tormented me no more. Already, she was one unlikely face among many. I was surprised at my sudden infatuation of the day before. How could I have felt such a blaze of passion for that pleasant little Englishwoman on her holiday?

"I don't care what you say, it's never this sunny in Asnières!"

Denise shielded her eyes with one hand, blinded by a ray of sunlight. I adjusted one of the shutters so as not to dazzle her. She lay naked on the bed, the cast-off sheets strewn over the floor.

"It's quite wonderful," she sighed, flinging her arms wide in the shape of a cross.

"What is?"

"This! The summer! The Côte, the sun… To think there are Eskimos in ice houses right now, and English people under umbrellas."

English people under umbrellas. I imagined Marjorie Faulks on Regent Street beneath a blue umbrella. I hoped desperately that she wouldn't go looking for my letter. And if she wrote to me, at any rate, I had determined not to write back. How could I have penned six pages of heated declarations to that unknown woman? I pictured her in my MG, and my initial irritation returned. With her sunburn, and seawater matting her hair, I had found her ugly. And detested her sharp, acid voice.

"Something on your mind, O man of my life?" Denise had been watching me.

"Nothing. Just drifting."

"You're drifting off without me. I think something's happened."

"What, an accident?"

"Nothing physical. In the mind, perhaps."

I dived three metres across the room and landed at her side on the bed. The springs gave a sinister twang. Kneeling beside Denise, I tapped her forehead, as if knocking on a door.

"Pardon me, my good woman, things are sounding a little hollow in there this morning! You're the one talking about accidents of the mind, when I feel so happy I could shout for joy."

"I know what I mean."

But I was quite sure I did not. Denise was never one to talk in riddles. She was spontaneous and direct, even when she was joking.

"You don't love me any more, Jean-Marie!"

"Is that a joke?" I asked quietly.

But in my heart of hearts, I was not proud.

"I wish it was!"

"If you can think such a thing, Denise, then I shall hate you.

You know very well I can't live without you. Yesterday life was unbearable, and this morning I feel like singing."

"What does that prove? You needed to make love to someone and you'd had enough of being alone. You see, the biggest difference between a man and a woman is psychological. A man is always amazed to discover that the woman he loves no longer loves him back. She has to announce it to him, and even then he will persist in believing she's making it up. Whereas a woman knows when her man has fallen out of love, even before he knows it himself."

She spoke solemnly, staring up at the ceiling, but her ironic smile played at the corners of her mouth.

"You little bitch!" I protested, getting up off the bed. "Anyone would think you were determined to ruin my day."

She held her lovely, sensual arms out to me.

"Come and forgive me, you handsome, selfish beast!"

For four days we behaved like a couple of kids revelling in sunshine and freedom. I have always loathed sentimental film scenes of couples chasing one another on the beach, rolling in the surf, like a photograph on some lurid poster! But images like these are the stuff of life. We struggle our whole lives to recreate corny calendar scenes: beaches, mountains, an ivy-clad cottage, children on a swing, a basketful of kittens. For four days, I didn't give a thought to Marjorie Faulks. She was lost somewhere inside me, like most of the women who had crossed my path before Denise.

It happened on the fifth day. We were coming down from our room, dressed for the beach, and Denise went to hang our key in its pigeonhole.

I waited in the hall, watching the maids lugging the bundles of laundry. The air smelt of warm petrol.

"Here! Some mail for you."

Denise came towards me, holding out a long, narrow envelope on the head of her badminton racket. The stamp bore the image of Queen Elizabeth II.

I felt a sudden rush of hatred for the slanting, thoroughly British hand, with its characteristic flourishes.

The foolish, emotive girl had found my letter and replied. I caught Denise's mocking, enquiring eye.

"Aren't you going to read it?"

"Whatever can this be?" I muttered, seizing the missive.

"The accident!" she answered, twirling her racket. "Don't play the hypocrite, Jean-Marie dear. The accident has written you a letter."

I wanted to object, take the upper hand. I felt ridiculous, but there was nothing I could say. I would put on a brave face. And stop staring at Denise in defeat and embarrassment. Angrily, I ripped at the envelope with my teeth and pulled out a letter torn in two. I held the pieces together and read:

> Perhaps you don't know London. But you've been dwelling here for three days…

Music has the power to change a mood in four beats. This opening phrase was like certain passages of Mozart. Immediately, an enchanting ode filled my heart and Marjorie's absence hit me like a fist in the throat. The lines danced before my eyes, and my hands trembled with emotion as I held the two parts of the letter.

Now I know what it means to belong to an island nation, Jean-Marie. I am in exile here. From you! And yet, I don't know you. I remember a look, a tone of voice, the colour of your skin in the hollow of your cheek…

"Has something happened?" Denise asked, urgently.

I shook my head. And yet something had happened, indeed.

"You're pale as death."

"Not at all!"

"Is it serious?"

"Wait, be quiet a minute…"

She left. I saw her lithe shadow stretching across the lobby's tiled floor. And then she vanished into the rectangle of light filling the entrance. Perhaps I should have run after her, but I didn't feel up to the task.

…I've got an English-French dictionary beside me. But I haven't opened it once, Jean-Marie. I find it so easy to write to you. I'm a bit like your little French saint who spoke about her visions in every language…

…I'm leaving for eight days in Scotland, on my own at first – my husband will be joining me next week. I'll be at the Learmonth Hotel in Edinburgh. You can write to me there if you still want to. You can find me there if…

The letter stopped dead. It wasn't even signed. She had chosen to end it there, with her appeal.

5

I thought Denise would be waiting for me in my MG, parked under a reed shelter near the hotel. But she wasn't there. I drove slowly in the direction of the beach. I followed our usual route, scouring the already-crowded pavements. I spotted Denise in the throng. She was wearing very short pale-blue shorts, covering nothing of her long, brown legs, and a kind of white towelling pinafore top, whiter than any white thing around it – dazzlingly white. Denise tapped her racket against her legs as she walked, hurrying along much faster than usual.

I drove two metres ahead of her and pulled over.

"Need a ride, pretty lady? You seem in a hurry."

A street sweeper clearing the gutter paused in his work and stared at me with outright admiration. Then he stared at Denise, wondering if she would "take the bait". She did. Wordlessly, impassively, she climbed into the passenger seat.

"Thanks," I muttered, driving off.

"I'm sorry."

This was unexpected from Denise. She hated apologizing, especially when she was in the wrong.

"Well, there's a surprise." I pushed my advantage. "Do you even know who was writing to me?"

"An Englishwoman you met when you first got here," she answered. "An Englishwoman who fell for your charms and can't get your nights of wild passion out of her mind."

She wasn't mocking me, exactly; there was just a hint of bitter jealousy. Denise had guessed everything. Nights of wild passion excepted.

"What happened doesn't deserve so much as the scowl on your face," I assured her, gently stroking her thigh.

I told her about meeting Marjorie. She seemed not to listen, staring intently at the other cars. We drove at a crawl, with long stops at the traffic lights. Newspaper vendors in striped swimming shorts sold the latest calamities to customers on café terraces. The air smelt of saffron and hot oil. Outside the arcade, children practised shooting electric rifles at bears scurrying in circles in a glass cage. When the "death ray" struck, the bears would stop in their tracks, rear up with a cavernous roar then pirouette on the spot and hurtle in the opposite direction. The crackle of gunfire and the din of the thunder-struck bears rose above the noise of the street. Denise stared at the creatures' clumsy toings and froings, against a forest scene worthy of the backdrop for a scout-hut pantomime. I was telling her about Marjorie, in what I felt was appropriately jocular fashion, but she appeared interested in nothing but this tawdry fairground game.

"So there's really nothing to make a scene about, you see?"

She turned to look at me. She had her own particular way of diving straight into my innermost thoughts. Then she took her sunglasses out of her bag and put them firmly on her nose. Not a word was spoken until we reached the beach.

Even the habitués at the bar of the Grand Café in some minor provincial capital have a less developed sense of ritual than the beach regulars of the Côte d'Azur. Entrenched habits are contracted faster at the seaside than anywhere else. Everyone clings fiercely to the same proud possessions: their spot, their parasol, their circle of shade, their sand and their deckchair. We were against the back wall of the beach, near the volleyball pitch. Our parasol was plain blue; our deckchairs too. The parasol was always closed when we arrived, and we never opened it straight away. Denise would anoint herself with Ambre Solaire. I would do her back before hurrying to the tap to wash my hands. I hated the feel of the filthy stuff. Next, we would spend a good hour frying gently in the sun. I read the newspaper while Denise supervised her tanning with scientific precision. Once she judged herself done to a turn, she would open the parasol and resume conversation in that lovely, languid voice that made me want her so badly.

That morning, I had forgotten to buy the newspaper, and our routine was disrupted. I tried to lose myself in the burning heat, to think of nothing at all, but Marjorie Faulks's letter danced in my head.

> Now I know what it means to belong to an island nation… I am in exile here. From you!

The volleyball players arrived, jostling one another as they ran. Magnificent young men, eyed by every woman on the beach. Denise had her particular favourite: a tall, handsome, dumb blond who strutted as if he had spent his entire life in front of a mirror. We called him Narcissus. Denise swore she would happily succumb. "Because he's a ravishing young brute," she explained, in her defence. She had always fantasized about making love to a labourer, or a docker. She said intellectuals ruined the act of love by complicating it.

"Did you see? Narcissus has yet another, different pair of shorts today," I whispered. She was lying flat on her stomach, on top of her still-folded deckchair. She lifted her head and half-opened one eye with that economy of gesture shown by intoxicated sun-worshippers everywhere. Then her eye closed, her head dropped once more, and she lay still for a long while. I gazed at the American warships anchored off-shore. They looked like something from another era, so close to the bathers. Motor boats buzzed. Skiers traced the horizon, infinitely close, with the mechanical haste of the fairground bears we had seen earlier.

"Did she write in English or French?"

I heaved a long sigh.

"Listen, Denise, you're not going to…"

"No, I'm not. Just so I know."

Her skin gleamed liked freshly polished walnut. She gave a little laugh.

"You and an Englishwoman. It's quite… hard to understand. Don't you think?"

I didn't think. I was gripped by fever. A full-blown attack – raging temperature, teeth chattering, icy sweat on my back.

I opened the parasol and lingered in its ruffled shade. I had come to an unexpected realization. This couldn't work any longer, Denise and me. We had nothing in common. The usual hubbub continued all around us. Sometimes, the volleyball landed at our feet, spraying us with sand.

Narcissus came to fetch the ball, prancing over the hot sand. The blond hairs on his tanned legs gleamed like threads of gold.

He shot me a disdainful look by way of a greeting and paused in front of Denise, the ball tucked under his arm, conquering and smug.

"How's the sun this morning?" he asked her, bringing his full powers of seduction to bear on this banal question.

Denise didn't open her eyes.

"Like you," she enunciated. "Getting in my eyes but leaving me cold."

The youth departed, cut to the quick, while his comrades roared and slapped their thighs.

"What was that for?" I objected.

"Just to be mean. I feel better now."

"Are you jealous?"

"Yes. Don't let it go to your head."

I took Marjorie's torn letter from the pocket of my shorts and tossed it under Denise's nose.

"Read it. You'll see."

"What will I see?"

I knew full well my gesture was pointless and in poor taste, but like every man who falls in love with a new woman, I needed her predecessor's opinion.

"I don't know, just read it!"

She read. Unhurriedly, holding the two halves of the letter in careful alignment. Her hands were perfectly steady.

I watched for her reaction, shielding my eyes with my hand, because the sun was shining straight into my face now.

When she had finished, Denise returned the letter to me.

"Odd sort of girl! Quite unusual for an Englishwoman, it seems to me. Interesting. Romantic, rather mysterious, but clearly very much hooked. It's always marvellous at first with people like her because they start out thinking you're quite wonderful."

I felt a sudden flare of anger.

"You're quite the psychologist!"

"I know what I'm talking about. They're in constant need of a hero, and so they find one. And then as time goes on they discover their romantic Ivanhoe is a respectable architect with a gentleman's club, carpet slippers and a tendency to sore throats; who has to shave every day, and likes veal stew. And so the illusion crumbles. It's perfectly normal."

She propped herself up on her elbows to get a better look at me.

"Do you need to be an Ivanhoe, *chéri*? Go on, admit it! Don't all men? That's why little girls like her are always half right, to start with. What will you do, go to Scotland?"

"Stop talking nonsense, will you?"

"But she's waiting, Jean-Marie. She's waiting – can't you read between the lines? You can't leave her in the lurch just because she's in Edinburgh and you're in Juan-les-Pins."

"Listen, Denise, if you don't shut up immediately I'll do something very… unpleasant."

She stared at my hands, clenched tight around the armrests of my deckchair, and gave a sad smile.

"Come and play badminton, it'll help you relax."

"It's not time!"

"Come on! A romantic hero doesn't need an allotted time!"

I played reluctantly, missing the shuttlecock at least every second stroke. I hated the ludicrous, feathery projectile twirling in the air between us.

A vigorous swipe from Denise sent it spiralling into the sky. I watched it twist and fall, endlessly down and down. My thoughts raced ahead. I told myself, "If I don't reach a decision by the time it hits the ground, it's all over." The shuttlecock hit the sand with a soft thud. I picked it up, but instead of hitting it back to Denise, I took it over to her.

"Come on," I muttered, "Let's go back. I'm leaving for Scotland."

She nodded.

I could see my decision came as no surprise.

"Poor Ivanhoe," she sighed. "You have no idea what fools heroes can be."

6

I arrived in London that same evening. I had hoped to take a flight to Edinburgh straight away, but a strike by cabin crews had just broken out and I was forced to take the train. At King's Cross station I was informed that there were a few places left on the night train to Edinburgh, but its departure time was unclear. The strike looked set to extend its grip. Some suburban trains had already stopped running, and walkouts had begun across the network. I booked a couchette nonetheless, pleading with the Almighty to let my train leave the station. I could think of nothing but Marjorie. I was obsessed, and my need to find her again became more and more urgent. It was powerful, wonderful and painful all at once. I was wildly happy and desperately sad. But my thoughts of Denise were dispassionate and detached. She had accompanied me to Nice airport in the MG.

When we parted, she said quietly:

"I'll stay here until the end of the month. If you aren't back by then, I'll take your car to Paris and park it in your garage."

Mechanically she proffered her lips. I kissed her swiftly and left.

My train was scheduled to leave at eleven o'clock in the evening. At 10.30, it was ready and waiting at the platform, but the sight of it inspired little confidence in the otherwise deserted station. A strange atmosphere prevailed. It reminded me of the war. Everything around me was silent and tense. A handful of black porters went about their business, escorting sullen passengers to their compartments without a sound. I left my case on my couchette and paced the grey concrete of the platform to calm my nerves. Walking the length of the train, I realized no locomotive was attached.

If the train failed to leave, I would take a room for the night and attempt to hire a car in the morning. How long would it take to reach Edinburgh? Perhaps two days. I knew how narrow and congested the roads were in England.

At a quarter to eleven, an engine pulled into the station, puffing and gasping and filling the immense terminus with its miraculous din. The train jolted with the shock of the buffers. At eleven o'clock precisely, we shuddered into life. I hardly dared rejoice, fearing a false start. But no, leaning on the window rail in the corridor, I watched the gloomy station hall recede into the distance, with its pale lights and curving lines of trolleys, like the truncated sections of a snake. Little by little, the giant clock faces dwindled to bright, inexpressive dots.

Damp, ugly suburbs drawn in shades of Indian ink shot past faster and faster beside the tracks. A piece of filthy grit caught in my eye and I wound up the window, reassured.

I was fast asleep when the steward rapped on my door. He was a tall, thin, disagreeable-looking man with a pointy face.

His burgundy jacket was filthy with soot. I realized all of a sudden that the train wasn't moving, and thought the gangling creature with his shifty, spy's expression was coming to tell me we were stuck in the middle of nowhere.

"Six o'clock, sir! Edinburgh in one hour!"

As if by magic, the train began moving again. The steward handed me a narrow tray set with a meagre breakfast: pale, tasteless coffee and a shortbread biscuit that disintegrated the moment I sank my teeth into it. The smell of stale sheets, rusty taps and soot, the grim landscape rolling by under sheets of rain, did nothing to quell my excitement. In one hour I would be in Edinburgh. I was going to join Marjorie Faulks. Her Ivanhoe! Denise was not mistaken: I was playing the hero all right, but a hero of a different sort, determined to offer Marjorie all the love and support she so plainly hoped from me.

Edinburgh station was scarcely more heartening than King's Cross, but its bustle was consoling in its way. A train coming in is always cheerier than a train pulling out. Coming straight from Juan-les-Pins, I had no raincoat. Standing in line for a taxi beneath the great glass roof, I felt idiotic in my lightweight clothes. My pearl-grey raw silk suit was far from ideal for the Scottish weather, even in August.

The station occupied an immense gully of sorts. When the taxi emerged from the ramp leading down to it, I discovered Edinburgh at a glance. Dark, austere and formidable, the castle on its black crag seemed to have risen up from the past. I think at that moment, I sensed a vague foreboding of the drama that would befall me there.

The taxi drove along Princes Street, Edinburgh's very own Champs-Elysées, a great, broad thoroughfare flanked with modern buildings along one side, and on the other by a steep valley transformed into public gardens. On the far side of the valley, the old city soared on its rocky crag, the jagged outline of its sinister, black castle rising from crenellated walls masking its antiquated artillery. The policemen looked nothing like their counterparts in London. They wore flat-topped caps and white overalls, like the employees of some transport company. I had hoped to find the entire population in kilts, but the passers-by wore poorly cut suits. They had a down-at-heel, but contented air.

My taxi left Princes Street and its shops to dip into another valley. We crossed a bridge and emerged onto a tree-lined road, not quite an avenue, nor merely a street, as such. Reddish-coloured double-decker buses followed one behind the other in obedience to some strange logic. The taxi turned sharply across the road and pulled up behind a luxurious Swedish coach. Immaculately groomed elderly ladies surrounded the vehicle, chattering animatedly, accompanied by a handful of infirm or senile old men.

I read the neon sign flickering wanly on the front wall of a forbidding edifice with all the charm of a municipal office block: Learmonth Hotel. She was here, in this great, blackened fortress. My heart leapt and knocked violently at my ribs. I trembled with emotion at the thought of our impending reunion.

As I made my way to the entrance, a Scotsman in a green kilt and a tall black fur hat stepped out to greet me. At first sight, I took him for a soldier. He wore a heavy cape thrown over one shoulder, and clasped a fat tartan bag firmly under one arm, bristling with black pipes. His kilt, cape and doublet, and the bag of his pipes were all cut from the same green-and-red chequered woollen cloth. The musician positioned himself in the hotel entrance and began to play a traditional tune. The Swedish tourists were enraptured, snapping photographs by the dozen. The nasal whine was an ode of welcome, it seemed. I stared at the hotel's austere façade, scrutinizing each window in hopes of seeing Marjorie's face. But the Learmonth's residents were clearly uninterested. The windows remained firmly shut.

When the musician had finished his piece he came towards me and took my luggage with confident authority. This was the hotel's porter – a fine, broad man with red hair and pale-blue eyes.

He led me into the reception area. In all my travels, I had never seen a hotel lobby like it. The floor was covered in strips of tartan carpet, each different from the next. The same was true of the wallpaper. The effect was crazy. A chameleon wandering into this multicoloured décor would have exploded on the spot. The hotel proprietor, on the other hand, was very like his opposite number in Juan-les-Pins, but chubbier, pinker, balder. He greeted me with an air of vague defiance, unsure what to make of a client who turns up at half past seven in the morning, without a reservation. With my tanned skin and flashy suit (clearly unwearable here in Edinburgh), I made a singularly "loud" impression.

He gave me a room, nonetheless, but asked me to wait as it would not be ready straight away. I was on the brink of asking him to call Marjorie, but held back at the last minute. Her husband would be joining her at this hotel, and I didn't want to compromise her good name. I left my case under a wall seat and waited for breakfast. After an hour, the hotel's residents began to come down, making their way to the dining room. They were mostly elderly, and I quickly understood that the Learmonth did the bulk of its business with tour operators, concluding furthermore that the cruise companies in question catered exclusively to widows, elderly spinsters and arthritic couples. More coaches were pulling up outside the hotel, and each time the piper shouldered his instrument and stepped out to greet the new arrivals with a dawn serenade. I felt increasingly impatient. How idiotic to have travelled so far, only to sit for hours in a hotel lobby, waiting for the woman I was desperate to find.

I entered the dining room and ordered bacon and eggs. The vast space looked like a boarding school refectory. Elderly American ladies cackled like frightened turkeys and laughed out loud at the slightest pretext. An old Texan with an extraordinary, broad-brimmed straw hat and an elaborate hearing aid stuffed into one ear sat eating porridge with a teaspoon. The gruel trickled down his hand-painted tie. A senile cowboy was a comical enough sight, but I felt no impulse to smile. I was worried. Something must have happened to Marjorie. The restaurant emptied. I was startled each time a woman walked close by my table. Soon I was alone with the waitresses in their white caps, pushing trolleys laden with dirty dishes.

I went back out to the multicoloured lobby. One wall bore a large wooden board covered in a criss-cross arrangement of tartan ribbons. The reception staff were distributing mail here, tucking letters behind the ribbons at random, to be retrieved by the residents. I searched frantically for Marjorie's name, certain I would not find it.

But there it was.

On the unopened telegram sent by me the day before, from Juan-les-Pins.

7

The little blue-and-white rectangle looked like some dreaded formal announcement. It spoke of Marjorie's absence with such poignant eloquence that it brought tears to my eyes.

Almost immediately, I decided that it was perhaps not my telegram after all. And so I committed a serious indiscretion. I opened the envelope. My disappointment was punishment enough for my boldness.

J'ARRIVE MON AMOUR
JEAN-MARIE VALAISE

The brief text, like a resounding cry of victory, had a sinister ring now. Filled with shame and despair, I folded the message into the envelope and tucked it back behind the tartan ribbon. No one had seen me. The hotel was busier than a bus station. Guests packed the lobby with their luggage, then poured outside to storm one of the waiting Pullman coaches. Others were piling in, to be greeted by the whine and moan of the bagpipes.

The manager spotted me and raised an arm. I hurried over, filled with sudden hope.

"Your room is ready for you now, sir."

That was all. The piper had picked up my bags already, and led me in the direction of the stairs. He went ahead of me, breathing heavily, like a lumberjack hard at work. His lungs seemed incapable of functioning unless he was blowing into one of the black teats on his monstrous udder-like instrument. His thick calves were covered in reddish hairs. A classic Scots dagger with an engraved silver pommel was tucked into one of his socks.

A clever architect could have carved a decent-sized apartment from the vast, inhuman dimensions of my room. The ceiling was some four metres high, and the window ledge was level with my chest; I would have felt more at home on the empty stage of the Paris Opera. Finding myself alone, I realized how a man can feel more imprisoned in a vast space than in a tiny cell. I felt crushed. The room's tartan carpet and gaudy wallpaper made me quite sick. I sank into an armchair and attempted to review my situation.

Marjorie Faulks must have postponed her visit to Scotland. Doubtless she had informed me, but I had left before receiving her letter. What could I do? Send a telegram poste restante to London, asking her to fix a rendezvous? I could see no other way to reach her. Then I sensed a new ray of hope: perhaps my telegram was late, and had been delivered to the Learmonth just that morning? Perhaps Marjorie was still sleeping, on the other side of the wall! Perhaps she hadn't collected her mail last night. She may not have reached Edinburgh yet. Her letter said she was travelling to Scotland, but not when. How quickly could she get here, with this transport strike threatening to spread? I went down to reception.

The tumult of the morning coaches had abated, and the lobby was empty. Behind the glass panels of the reception desk, the proprietor was drinking a cup of tea.

"Excuse me," I asked. "Is there a Mrs Marjorie Faulks, from London, among your guests?"

He dipped a biscuit into his tea and nibbled at it. When the biscuit was finished, he responded with an evasive shrug before running his tongue carefully around his gums and consulting the hotel register.

"When would she have arrived?"

"Two days ago, at the most."

He ran his finger quickly down the long columns of names and came to a halt on the final, blank page.

"No, sir. Nobody of that name."

"In that case, you must have an advance booking from a Mrs Faulks."

He pushed the book towards me; I thought he wanted me to check the list myself, but he was inviting me to add my own name and address. I took the opportunity to double-check the entries for the last two days, which annoyed him greatly. His bright expression darkened.

"Would you mind checking your advance bookings?" I asked quietly.

He opened a much smaller book and consulted it briefly.

"Is the lady on an organized tour?"

"No, I don't believe so."

"I have no individual bookings, sir."

"But there's a telegram for her!" I protested.

I pointed to the board. The telegram had disappeared.

Panic-stricken, I checked every letter and note. Had I slipped the cable behind another envelope? I lifted each of them, one by one. The hotel owner liked this not one bit, and showed his displeasure by joining me in front of the board.

"Ten minutes ago there was a telegram here for Mrs Marjorie Faulks," I declared forcefully. "Who distributes the mail?"

"I do, sir."

"You must remember the telegram, it arrived yesterday..."

"Several telegrams arrived yesterday, sir."

His cheeks reddened and his stare intensified.

"Look here, try to remember."

"My hotel is a popular tour destination, sir. I have no time to remember each guest by name. Over a hundred people arrive every day, and they leave the following morning. We display the mail, but we do not check names."

He looked fit to burst. I tried soothing him with a contrite smile.

"Of course! I understand. I'm so sorry. But the fact remains, the telegram in question was right here less than fifteen minutes ago. Who took it, if not Mrs Faulks?"

The logic of this appealed to the hotel proprietor's rational cast of mind. He poked his tongue behind his bottom lip, stretching the skin. He was freshly shaven and smelt of soap.

"Well, sir, I imagine that the lady in question had planned to stay at my hotel. But the Learmonth was fully booked last night. So she went elsewhere and came by this morning to collect her mail. These things happen."

I could have hugged him. Obviously! He was right!

"You were in reception just now. Did you see a young woman with reddish, chestnut-coloured hair?"

"The hall was full of people, sir. Did you see her yourself?"

"And what about yesterday? You can't have missed her if she came to ask about a room?"

He reflected on this, sticking his tongue firmly into his right cheek.

"I don't remember seeing any young lady, sir. But I don't spend all day on reception. I'll ask my wife when she comes down."

"Thank you."

A side table was piled with leaflets about Edinburgh. One listed all of the city's main hotels. I took it and went out.

The rain had just stopped, and a timid sun made the streets shine in the pale, soft northern light. I waited for a taxi but none came. I settled for a bus to take me to the centre of town.

I enquired at every hotel in the leaflet. The search took over three hours, to no avail. No one had seen or heard of Marjorie Faulks. The mystery defeated me; I was dead with fatigue. This whole adventure was a monstrous farce.

I hoped for news back at the Learmonth, but no one had asked for me, and the owner's wife – a small, brown-haired woman with a distracted, disapproving air – was quite certain no young woman answering Marjorie's description had requested a room the day before. The name Faulks meant nothing to her either.

8

A nightmarish day!

Lost and bewildered, I wandered past the shop windows on Princes Street, gazing indifferently at their meagre displays. Everything looked ugly and grim: the items on show, the passers-by, the buildings, the weather. The rain fell in sudden, sporadic bursts, but there was no brightening of the sky in between.

The swollen clouds gurgled like overworked drains. Nothing distracted me from my plight, not even the tartan-clad soldiers slowly pacing the pavements.

In Princes Street Gardens, at the bottom of the valley separating the old part of the city from the new, a band played traditional songs while a great many couples danced. Most were in national dress, distinguished only by their different-coloured tartans. People out for a stroll gathered on the nearby seats to watch. At the edge of the stage, a portly woman with the air of a girl scout called instructions into a microphone, in a gravelly, stentorian voice.

Vivid, close-cropped lawns, dotted with flower beds, extended either side of the open-air theatre. People disported themselves here whenever the rain let up, spreading their raincoats on the neatly mown grass. Lovers lay close together, embracing in full view of passers-by on the narrow tarmac paths.

By eight o'clock in the evening, the weather was almost fine. Suddenly, the clouds cleared and the light was so bright it might have been three o'clock in the afternoon. I was half dead with hunger, and stepped into a restaurant. The place was on two levels. For dinner, only the first-floor dining room was open. I settled myself at a small table beside a bay window, overlooking the whole of Princes Street.

Sunlight sparkled on the lawns and gilded the battlements of the citadel. Why was Marjorie not here, sitting opposite me? What had happened? Who had taken my telegram from the board at the Learmonth?

A surly, ugly, elderly waitress took my order. Fresh salmon, and lamb with mint sauce. The food was tasteless and the fried potatoes accompanying the lamb were almost raw. I doused everything in ketchup and convinced myself it was edible. My fellow diners were a lifeless lot, drab and silent; when the demands of service forced them to speak, they did so in a church whisper. I began to detest their presence, and chose instead to gaze out at the great prospect of Princes Street, with its parade of buildings, the double-decker buses plying its broad thoroughfare, and the sloping gardens, at the bottom of which the tartan-clad couples were still dancing their complicated quadrilles. The passengers on the upper decks of the buses were a distraction in an otherwise sombre, imposing scene. Level with my gaze, their stately passage reminded me of the bears in their glass case in Juan-les-Pins. Princes Street was a major artery, filled with traffic. The buses came relentlessly, one after another, as if emerging from their depot first thing in the morning. All at once, I started in shock. There, sitting at the front of a wine-red bus, was Marjorie. I leapt to my feet like a madman, spilling my beer bottle on the tablecloth. Pressed against the bay window, I waved in desperation, but we were separated by the breadth and bustle of Princes Street, and she could not see me, though the bus was halted at a red light.

She wore a black raincoat with a glossy sheen, like sealskin, and her hair was knotted in a velvet ribbon. The sight of her was torture.

There I was, barely ten metres from her, and quite unable to attract her attention! Her bus pulled away. There was no time to pay my bill, run downstairs and chase after the lumbering vehicle. A taxi? A glance down at the street told me none were stationed nearby. I had the presence of mind to note the number of the bus: 12.

I watched as it drove away. In the distance its rounded back end resembled a giant beetle. The waitress mopped my spilt beer with vehement disapproval. Her red-rimmed eyes were grey, with sparse, stubby lashes that fluttered when she felt she was being watched. The profound silence in the restaurant was, I realized, targeted at me. I recovered my composure and asked for the bill. The waitress took delight in presenting it only after a considerable lapse of time.

Now the shops were closed, the traffic had eased, and Princes Street was sunk in Sunday evening torpor. It was broad daylight, with a clear sky and bright sunshine, but the city had gone to sleep. The tall blackened buildings looked like gigantic mausoleums. There was no one at the open-air theatre, and no more tourists visible on the castle esplanade. It was as if an air raid warning had sent people scurrying to their cellars. The effect was unnerving, like the certainty of an imminent threat whose precise nature is unknown.

I reached the nearest bus stop; almost every route serving the city passed through this nerve centre, and the pavement was lined with numbered posts, marking their stops. I located the number 12, near a crossroads, and prepared to wait.

After about ten minutes, a virtually empty vehicle came along. I stayed standing on the rear platform, beside the conductor, who remarked that it was a "lovely" evening. But I was in no mood for conversation, and replied that I didn't understand English.

The bus hurtled up and down the Edinburgh hills. I rode along broad, silent thoroughfares, staring hard at the windows piercing the dark, cliff-like buildings in hopes of discovering Marjorie's refuge. Knowing that she was in Edinburgh ought to have filed me with delight, but I was half dead with anxiety. When I spotted her on the top deck of the bus, my only thought had been to attract her attention. But now, reliving the scene after the heat of the moment, I was struck by how exhausted she had looked. I had glimpsed her for just thirty seconds, from a distance, but her anxious expression had been plain to see. *I knew something bad had happened to her.* Something that had forced a change of plan. Where was she now? I wanted to retrace the number 12 bus route on foot, hollering her name every ten metres. The farther the huge bus drove, the greater my state of panic.

We were moving through a drab, outlying district of factories, gasworks and increasingly squat buildings. Shops were few and far between. A set of railway tracks emerged suddenly from a large gateway, crossing the street into a factory yard.

The number 12 came to a halt. I thought we had reached another stop, but the remaining passengers all alighted:

shabby-looking men in old-fashioned caps. Each carried a metal mess tin, and every red-veined face was painted grey with fatigue.

"Terminus, sir."

9

I returned to the city centre on foot, retracing the route of the number 12 bus. There were seven stops between my point of embarkation and the terminus. I appealed to an imaginary sixth sense to determine where Marjorie had stepped down.

I discounted the last three: the neighbourhoods were too run-down by far. Once the buildings were smarter and better maintained, I paid careful attention to each façade, hoping for a hotel that might have escaped my morning tour. I found only one, more a family-run guesthouse, but I rang at the door nonetheless. It was opened, fearfully, by an elderly lady with blue hair and thick glasses that gave her a frog-like air. The place was fully booked, she informed me. I asked whether a Mrs Marjorie Faulks was staying with her, and was assured she wasn't.

The remainder of the journey was an ordeal. Now I was interested not only in the buildings lining the route, but the side streets too. It was tiring, and it was dispiriting. I was under no illusion as to the likely outcome of my search. A young woman can't be sniffed out, just like that, on the deserted streets of Edinburgh, at ten o'clock at night. The forbidding tenement blocks loomed darker, and more oppressive still, as night stole over the city. The sky was still bright, but the street lamps were lit. A North Sea wind blew along the steep streets, each gust spattering volleys of raindrops on the greasy pavements; not proper rain, but flecks of spray snatched from the not-so-distant waves.

My stony solitude was hopeless now. The high walls that harboured Marjorie would not release her to me tonight.

At the Learmonth Hotel, the owner's wife was reading a paperback novel in the lobby. All was quiet. The bagpiper, in shirt-sleeves now, was unpacking a consignment of ginger wine; the red-topped bottles clustered around him in rows, like skittles.

I asked for my key. I couldn't remember my room number; the owner's wife checked her register.

"Someone called for you!" she announced.

I started in surprise.

"Mrs Faulks?"

"No, a man."

I was astounded.

"What sort of man?"

"I don't know, he called on the telephone."

"Was he French?"

"No, sir."

"What was his name?"

"He didn't leave a name, sir."

"Did he leave a message?"

"Nothing."

"Did he say he would call back?"

"He did not."

She handed me my key. I was in room 14.

I couldn't leave the conversation there. The mystery held me transfixed.

"This gentleman, Madame, did he… Did he ask for me by name?"

She looked surprised.

"Well of course, sir."

"He wanted to speak to me?"

"Well... he wanted to know if you had arrived at the hotel."

"What time did he call?"

"Sometime this afternoon, I couldn't say exactly when."

I hesitated to enquire further. Since my arrival, I seemed to have irritated the entire Scottish nation. Earlier that evening, through her monstrous glasses, the old lady with blue hair had displayed the same look of polite disapproval. And before that, the restaurant waitress mopping my spilt beer had made it quite clear I did not belong. Even the conductor on the number 12 bus had pronounced his "Terminus, sir" in tones laden with suspicion. And yet people like me readily enough, as a rule. This was another mystery altogether.

I bought an English newspaper from one of the piles on the reception desk. An ominous headline announced a general transport strike across the whole of Great Britain.

I was a prisoner in Edinburgh for the unforeseeable future.

I woke to bright sunlight in my room and thought for a moment that I was back in Juan-les-Pins. The sensation was so strong that I found myself reaching for the right-hand side of the bed, and the touch of Denise. But Denise was fast asleep, two thousand kilometres from here.

It was barely seven o'clock and, miraculously for Edinburgh, a beautiful summer's day was breaking. Through the vast, terrifying window, beyond the blackened rooftops, I beheld a cloudless Mediterranean sky, and concluded that this whole business would work itself out, the mysteries would be solved, and Marjorie would be in my arms before the morning's end.

Outside in the street, the bagpiper's nasal whine could be heard already, announcing the arrival of a fresh coachload of tourists. I took a shower and ordered a pot of black coffee. I had no desire to confront the elaborately groomed old ladies in the dining room.

One hour later, bright and ready for the day, brimming with energy and hope, I climbed aboard a number 12 bus on Princes Street.

The vehicle was thronged with passengers now. The city was full of a kind of muted joy that morning, agreeably solid, no longer the brutish, dark pile that had lowered my spirits the day before, but a picturesque ancient citadel, proud of its past and facing the future. Rather than ride "backwards" on the bottom platform, seeing the street names once they had passed, I climbed the stairs to the top deck and was lucky enough to find the exact seat that Marjorie had occupied the day before. Seen from above, the streets were an entertaining spectacle. I could observe the life of the tenement buildings, too. I searched again for a hotel I might have missed the night before, but there were no others along the route.

Through tall windows, I saw bare-chested men, and women in dressing gowns. I immersed myself in solemn and fanciful interiors – fleeting images gathered here and there, but they fed my growing awareness of the city. Uniformed delivery men placed milk bottles on doorsteps. Red mail vans the colour of fire engines zigzagged from one side of the street to the other. On their polished doors the gilded arms of Elizabeth II glittered fresh and bright in the sunshine. Passengers called out to one another, exchanging the same cheery phrase: "Lovely day today!"

The sunshine intoxicated them like cheap, heady wine. At every stop, the same sign was repeated over the tops of doors: *Bed and Breakfast*. I had not noticed this before. The revelation was like a shaft of light: travellers to Edinburgh could stay not only in hotels, but in private houses. People rented out part of their home, just as they do in the most popular parts of France. A bed for the night, and breakfast the following morning!

I stepped down from the bus. I was three stops beyond Princes Street. I should have turned back and begun a systematic search, visiting every bed and breakfast from the start of my route. But I was too impatient.

I rang at the first door I saw, bearing the now familiar sign. A tall, horse-faced man came to open it.

"Excuse me, sir, would you have a guest by the name…"

I rang at fifteen or so houses. This was no time of day to be calling at private addresses, as was made abundantly clear: the owners were eager to rent out their deceased parents' or soldiering son's bedroom, but they were quick to shut their door in my face with a brusque "No Mrs Faulks here, sir!"

If I continued from door to door, I would soon be singled out across Edinburgh. But my obstinate quest was not without a certain heady fascination: all those early-morning interiors, their panelled hallways full of copper plant holders and old prints. Bathrooms gurgled and sleepy children wailed. Sometimes, through a gap in a door, I glimpsed the wary features and tousled hair of the lady of the house.

"No, sir, I've nobody by the name of Mrs Faulks!"

In one house, a tiny, surly pug greeted me with a ferocious volley of barking. His mistress was forced to restrain him by the collar, or he would have thrown himself at me as I framed my question yet again.

I was conducting my search in reverse, heading back towards Princes Street. If Marjorie was staying at a bed and breakfast, she would have chosen a house close to the centre of town.

I kept count at first, but quickly lost track of the number of houses I had visited.

The building before me now was a large house showing traces of past finery. The steps leading to the front door were much wider than elsewhere, and flanked by two sparkling copper lamp posts. The sign offering rooms to let was tiny and difficult to see. The proprietor – or, more likely, the proprietress – was clearly diffident about the need to supplement her income in this way. I imagined an elderly lady facing ruin, or a dignified widow determined to keep hold of a residence that was now beyond her means.

I rang the bell. Almost immediately, the sound of galloping feet was heard in the hallway beyond, culminating in a dull thud that made the door frame shake. A key rattled in the lock, turned by an unsteady hand, and the heavy, iron-clad door swung open to reveal a charming small boy with blond, curly hair, looking me over from bottom to top with intense interest.

An elderly lady with an affected, sing-sing voice called out from somewhere in the house.

"Could you ask them to wait a moment, David? I'll be along instantly!"

David nodded in response. I smiled, but he remained grave and attentive.

The hall was a respectable size, suggesting an equally sizeable house. It was painted white, with a stone-flagged floor partly concealed under still-resplendent rugs. A gallery ran around the top, framed by a finely turned wooden balustrade. Suddenly, a door opened on the first floor, doubtless leading to one of the bathrooms. I looked up expecting to see the elderly lady whose voice I had just heard, but it was Marjorie who stepped out onto the landing. She was wearing a white bathrobe, with a towel knotted around her head. She started upon seeing me and I thought she would cry out in surprise. At the same time, the hostess emerged from one of the downstairs rooms.

She was not as old as I had expected, with a dumpy figure and heavy make-up. She wore a gaudily coloured dress, and held me firmly in the sights of an old-fashioned lorgnette. Everything happened at once, on two different levels. The proprietress gratified me with a nod after inspecting me through her eye-glass, and Marjorie, plainly horrified, gestured eloquently for me to ignore her completely.

"How may I be of help, sir?"

"Do you have any vacancies?"

"Alas, no!"

Upstairs, Marjorie had disappeared into her room, and I thought I could just make out the sound of voices.

"Then pardon me, Madame."

"Oh, you're French!"

"Yes."

"I'm really very sorry, but we're full…"

She concluded with an affable smile, fondling the little boy's head. For the first time since my arrival in Edinburgh, someone had softened towards me, quite spontaneously. I flashed a winning smile. She had given Marjorie a room, and there could be no higher virtue in my eyes. I bowed my way out of the hall with due ceremony. The proprietress was visibly disarmed.

Out on the street, I crossed to the other side to get a better look at the façade. I saw Marjorie's small, anxious face at a window on the first floor. She stared at me, motionless. She seemed crushed, somehow, and oppressed. What could have happened? Someone must have spoken to her from another part of the room: she turned to answer. I risked attracting attention if I remained planted outside on the pavement.

I walked away slowly, looking desperately for a hiding place where I could watch the house without being seen. But the street was lined by private houses with no porches. I walked a hundred metres but found nowhere to conceal myself. I reached the crossroads. Here, the quiet neighbourhood shook itself out of its slumber and came hesitantly to life. I bought a newspaper from a street vendor. The big, printed pages offered a screen of sorts – flimsy, but better than nothing.

I stepped into a patch of shade, to wait. I could see Marjorie's house from the crossroads. Close by, a clock tower struck nine.

10

After fifteen minutes, the newspaper vendor – a little old man wearing a vastly oversized fisherman's smock – began staring at me in surprise. A man on the lookout does not behave like a man merely waiting. I worried him slightly. I watched as he engaged a customer in conversation. The man turned and fixed me with a hostile stare. With my tanned complexion and raw silk suit, I was about as inconspicuous as a fly in a bowl of milk. If I continued my surveillance for much longer, I could find myself in trouble.

Half an hour went by, then an hour. I trembled with nerves. The old vendor was staring at me continuously now. I checked the street names, then walked over to where he stood.

"Excuse me," I asked, in a low voice. "Would you have seen a French car parked here just now, before I arrived? Two of my compatriots told me to meet them at the corner of East London Street, and they don't seem to be anywhere near arriving."

The newspaper vendor gave me a contrite smile, with an abundance of stubby, rotten teeth.

"Not seen nothing, sir."

"I've an idea they've stood me up. I'll wait a while longer, though. It's their first time in Edinburgh and they may have—"

I broke off. A couple was approaching on the opposite pavement, and the woman was Marjorie. She made commendable efforts not to look in my direction, but I could see she had spotted me. Her companion was a tall, thin man in a dark suit and a broad-brimmed, grey felt hat. A camera in a leather case knocked at his ribs. They stopped at the street corner, and Marjorie darted across the road to buy a newspaper. I watched from the corner of my eye as she quite deliberately dropped a screwed-up piece of paper. She went back to her companion and the couple walked away. I placed my foot over the paper, not daring to pick it up straight away in front of the newspaper vendor.

"What make of French car?"

I stared uncomprehendingly at the little man. He was unshaven, and his red beard was fading to white. He smelt bad. The collar of his smock shone with grease, as if it had been waxed.

"I'm sorry?"

"Your friends' car?"

"A Citroën. Do you know it?"

"Of course. You see quite a few around here."

I let my newspaper fall to the ground and stooped to pick up the ball of paper. It was still warm from being clenched tight in Marjorie's hand.

I walked a few metres then unfolded it with trembling fingers.

> Dear Jean-Marie,
>
> Thank you, thank you, thank you.
>
> Thank you for being here. Alas, I'm with my husband. I'll explain. Be in Princes Street Gardens near the bandstand this evening at 5.
>
> *Je vous aime.*
>
> "Your *Ma Jolie*"

Seized with emotion, childishly I pressed the piece of paper to my heart.

Je vous aime! Written in her own words.

The couple was still in sight, at the end of East London Street. I felt the urge to chase after them, seize Marjorie by the arm and lead her firmly away with me.

To kill time, I did something rather ridiculous for a man in my situation: I took a tour of the city aboard a special coach crammed full of British tourists. The driver was a solidly built, very old man with a shiny complexion and gold-rimmed glasses, delivering his own commentary into a microphone affixed to his chest. He paused the vehicle in front of houses once occupied by people whose names he recited with emphasis, none of whom meant anything to me.

When his explanations ran into extraneous detail, he would rise and turn to face the passengers, surveying his small world like a school prefect keeping a wary eye on an unruly band of pupils. Unlike most tourist guides, he seemed to know what he was talking about and was keen for us to take an interest. And so I visited the principal sights of Edinburgh: the castle, Mary Stuart's royal palace, the cathedral, Parliament House and a host of other places, doubtless all worthy of interest but which left me yawning with tedium.

By four o'clock in the afternoon I was on Princes Street. I passed through an iron gate leading to the gardens and walked down the sloping path to the lawns. The valley separating the old and new cities was filled with cool, sweet air. The lawns smelt of fresh grass. They had been mown and raked with such care that – to use a schoolboy cliché – they looked like expanses of baize. Neat flower beds, clipped and tended to remove every last wilting, withered petal, formed geometric patterns in the centre of the burgeoning greens. Broad, neatly trimmed paths wound their way through the spacious park in artful curves. The weather was fine, and there were more people about than the previous day. Scruffy-looking children drank at the fountains, splashing passers-by. On the stage of the open-air theatre, the fat lady was setting up her microphone. Couples in national costume were arriving, ready to dance.

Girls in white or blue dresses wore fine wool sashes pinned to one shoulder, in their clan colours. Musicians in threadbare dinner jackets stood chatting around a grand piano. I spotted a stone bench near the theatre, a short distance from the ticket booth. An old gentleman in a bowler hat was drinking tea from a cardboard cup. The thermos flask and packet of biscuits placed beside him only served to heighten the effect of a weary clown performing his sad routine.

His nose was veined with purple, his lower eyelids were sagging and red, and his hands shook.

"Lovely day, sir."

"Lovely day!" I agreed.

Yes, it was a fine day indeed. A day to delight the people of Scotland. Some had doubted it, and were out strolling now with raincoats or umbrellas on their arms.

The musicians took their places behind the music stands and tuned their instruments. The lady announcer spoke a few words, and the band struck up – a simple but lively tune with a brisk pace. The dance began. Gradually, passers-by filled the seats.

I gazed desperately around me as five o'clock approached. I could see no sign of Marjorie and feared she may have been prevented from coming at the last minute.

Then, exactly as this morning, there they both were, though I had not seen them arrive. He was guiding her by the arm, hurrying her towards the theatre entrance. I caught Marjorie's eye and thought I saw a confused apology, and a promise. Something – I have no idea what – alerted Mr Faulks: he turned sharply before pushing through the turnstile. And, straight away, he fixed his eyes on me, dazzling but cold as glass. It lasted a mere fraction of a second, but I felt he knew who I was, and what I was doing there. Then the Faulkses were swallowed up into the crowd.

I had no idea what I should do. I was an adolescent boy once more, sighing in turmoil and dread before a married woman's door. The fact was, I had been behaving like a lovelorn kid for the past several days.

The old man in the bowler hat poured himself a fresh cup of tea and ate a couple of biscuits, humming the band's tune as he munched.

"Do you like the Scottish dancing, sir?" he asked me, during a break in the music.

"Madly."

"Ah! It's a fine tradition. A warrior tradition."

"A fine, warrior people!" My hint of irony went undetected.

"Aye, that indeed we are, sir! Can I offer you a cup of tea?"

"No, thank you, I'm not a tea-drinker, myself."

The old man looked as if he might toss his cup of hot liquid in my face. But there was no time to enjoy his comical outrage. Marjorie had just left the theatre, alone. She did not walk in my direction, but shot me a glance, urging me to follow her. She walked quickly, her head sunk between her shoulders like an escaped convict caught in a searchlight. She reached a broad, sloping lawn behind the theatre stage. I caught up with her. She was waiting, motionless, arms hanging loosely at her sides, eyes closed, quite unable to move. I took her in my arms and pressed her close against me, sighing:

"At last…"

I had never felt such true, fierce, total happiness. Her heart was beating violently, to my alarm.

"Oh, Jean-Marie!" she breathed, opening her eyes, "you're far more handsome and strong than I remember."

Then she held me at arm's length in a gesture more tender still than my embrace.

"He knows everything, Jean-Marie."

I was bathed in the serene light of pure happiness, but here was a revelation calculated to bring me back down to earth.

"How so?"

"He was supposed to join me here in eight days. But at the last minute, he wanted to surprise me, and said he was coming too."

She spoke in quick bursts, shooting terrified glances all around her.

"I have to hurry. He thinks I've gone to the Ladies' toilet. If ever he…" Then she continued her story:

"We arrived the day before yesterday. The Learmonth was fully booked, do you see?"

I saw only too well, and began to glimpse what was coming next.

"So we went to a bed and breakfast he had heard of. Yesterday, he went to the hotel without telling me, while I was in the bathroom, and he found your telegram."

"Why did he do that? Did he suspect something?"

"A jealous man will always suspect something. And I suppose I haven't been myself since coming home from France. That's why he wanted to accompany me here, in fact."

"So what—?"

"No, I must go back to him, Jean-Marie, I must!"

"But my telegram… What did he say?"

"He showed it to me and asked me what it meant."

"And what did you tell him?"

"The truth, what else could I tell him?" Marjorie stammered, burying her forehead in my chest.

"And his reaction?"

"Nevil doesn't react. A snake shows more emotion. A snake will lash out and bite its prey, at least. Nevil is a snake with no bite. It's terrible, Jean-Marie! What will become of me!"

I kissed her slowly, with all my heart.

"We're going to leave, darling."

"But he won't let me… Now I have to go, I absolutely must. I'll meet you here, on this same lawn, tomorrow, same time."

She kissed me fleetingly on the lips. Then she hurried off in the direction of the theatre. But she had gone barely a dozen paces before she turned back, with a contrite expression.

"I'm so sorry, Jean-Marie: do you have a penny? To get back into the theatre: there are no tickets, just the turnstiles… And he's taken all the money I had in my bag."

She was red with shame, as if asking for a vast sum.

I took out a penny coin, kissed the effigy of George VI and slipped it into the palm of her hand.

"Do you need a few pounds, Marjorie, in case—"

"No! Oh no! Thank you. If he found that, he would know straight away."

When she had gone, I stretched out on the lawn with my arms flung wide, as I had done on the beach at Juan-les-Pins.

And just as in Juan, my head was bathed in bright sunshine.

11

The next morning, I packed my things at the Learmonth and cleared out. My sudden departure was not prompted by terror of Nevil Faulks. I did not fear him and would happily have smashed his face. But it seemed wiser, for Marjorie's safety, to let her husband believe I had returned home to France.

He had called the hotel once already to confirm my presence in Edinburgh, and he would very probably call again. If he discovered I had left, he would lower his guard and we would be better able to organize our own escape, Marjorie and I. I was determined to take her away with me, have her divorce Faulks, and marry her. My love for her was so complete that no other possible solution presented itself.

I explained to the proprietor of the Learmonth that I had met some fellow countrymen and was taking advantage of their car to get back to London, there being no end in sight to the transport strike.

I was certain this information would be repeated to Faulks. My only nagging doubt concerned Marjorie's reaction if her husband told her I had left. I feared she would take it for cowardice, rather than mere caution, and my fear sharpened my impatience to see her again on the lawn in Princes Street Gardens.

I took my things to a less grand, but more central hotel. The establishment was run by a brother and sister: hard-working, respectable folk. He resembled a curate, and she… a curate's sister. The hotel's only maid bore an uncanny resemblance to a curate's housekeeper.

I spent the day reading the red leather-bound Bible prominently displayed on my bedside table. From time to time, I stroked the mane of Pug, the little toy lion, whispering to him that he would soon be back with his mistress.

At five o'clock in the afternoon I was on the lawn, my heart beating hard and fast. Would Marjorie be able to get away? Had she formed a plan to calm her husband's all-seeing jealousy?

At ten minutes past five she appeared, walking quickly along the broad winding path. She wore a pale-blue two-piece suit in a light fabric – the afternoon was as warm as the day before. The suit flattered her youthful figure, and her face bubbled with freckles.

"Let's go farther away," she said, in greeting.

In the open-air theatre, the band played the same old-fashioned tunes as the day before. We could hear the fat announcer's mannish voice calling out instructions to the dancers, as they clapped along to their quadrille in near-perfect unison.

She took me by the hand and led me farther off, to a quieter part of the gardens, where the lawn swept round in a curve. The park-keepers had cut away the turf to prepare a huge flower bed, but nothing had been planted yet.

"I was afraid I wouldn't see you, Marjorie."

"I did promise."

"What about your husband?"

"He had a meeting with a colleague in Edinburgh, at a building site; he couldn't take me with him, so he ordered me to stay in our room."

"Did he call the Learmonth?"

"I don't know. He hardly speaks to me."

I told her that I had left the hotel, and why. She listened, nodding her head.

"You did the right thing, Jean-Marie. He may well have called there, in fact."

"We're leaving, Marjorie."

She fixed me with the grave look of a student trying hard to understand; her eyes filled with tears.

"Are you serious?"

"More serious than I've ever been about anything, my darling. Will you refuse to come?"

"Oh! Jean-Marie…"

Moving as one, we sat down in the lush grass.

"We barely know one another," she objected.

"Precisely. We have our whole lives to make each others' acquaintance, my darling."

Then she kissed me. And I returned her embrace. We were oblivious to everything around us. The lawn felt like a cloud floating two thousand metres up in a clear summer sky.

"You've suffered a great deal with that man, haven't you?"

"Yes," she answered. "But I prefer not to talk about that right now. Later, I'll tell you everything."

Her reticence gave the measure of her pain. Genuine distress lacks the strength and courage to express itself. It takes reserves of energy to confide. Marjorie had no reserves on which to draw. I had come into her life just as she was about to give up all hope and succumb to a living death: the appalling indifference endured by wives who are resigned to their fate.

"Where shall we go?" she asked, shyly.

"Paris, of course."

"But when? Travel is impossible right now. There are no trains, no planes. Not even passenger ferries. It's a general strike, and people say it will hold."

"I'll hire a car."

She shook her head.

"Yesterday, Nevil tried to hire one from Hertz: they hadn't a single vehicle left!"

This was vexing, indeed. I thought hard, stroking Marjorie's hand.

"*Vous savez—*"

"Jean-Marie," Marjorie interrupted me, in English. "Please, call me *tu*, not *vous*. I should love it. We make no distinction in English, anyhow."

"That won't be difficult. You've been *tu* in my thoughts from the very beginning."

Another, still more passionate kiss sealed our pact.

"Listen, the local services are all operating. We'll take a bus to the very edge of town, and once we're out of Edinburgh we'll find a discreet inn where we can sit out this damned strike."

I pictured the inn in my mind's eye: a fine old house with a slate roof, covered in ivy. I imagined the dining room, with its polished woodwork and monumental chimneypiece.

"What do you say?"

I was seized with sudden terror that she might refuse to see the whole adventure through. But she agreed with a firm nod of the head, signalling her determination.

"I'll go to my hotel," I said, "and fetch my things. Meanwhile you'll need to buy yourself some clothes. Going back to East

London Street is out of the question. Then you'll send a message to your husband telling him that you're leaving with me and that you plan to seek a divorce… Yes?"

She made no reply. She was staring at something behind me. Something in her fixed gaze prompted me to look around. I found myself staring at a pair of trousered legs planted firmly on the lawn, fifty centimetres behind my back. Far above loomed the white, ice-cold face of Nevil Faulks.

12

I was reminded of a motor accident that I was involved in eight years before, while driving along a corniche road. I was at the wheel of a Renault 4CV. I'd had the engine specially tuned and could take her to 130 kmph, to the astonishment of other motorists. We were four friends, all mad for speed, and I was going full tilt when we suffered a burst tyre. I lost control of the little car, which went into a tremendous swerve before heading straight for the cliff edge.

Nobody cried out on board. We were speechless with horror, ecstasy and acceptance of our fate. And then the car hit a boundary stone just so, and stopped right where it was, with no one injured. A miracle!

At the time, I felt a kind of vague disappointment. I felt cheated, in some obscure way – I had understood and accepted my imminent death, but death had not come.

Faulks's face was the car spinning out of control. The revolver in his hand was the ravine. Marjorie and I were the helpless passengers hurtling towards the abyss. We made no sound. Death had stepped aboard our cloud, and we could do nothing but submit to His coming.

Far below, the band was playing an old-fashioned mazurka of sorts, while the lady with the microphone urged her charges on, hollering quasi-military commands.

Couples frolicked on the lawns nearby. Their obliviousness seemed utterly inhuman. This man was about to kill us, to the general indifference of all. I remembered a cartoon I once saw, of a hanged man in the middle of a crowded public park. No one had noticed him.

No one in Princes Street Gardens had noticed a jealous husband pointing a gun at his wife and her accomplice.

Nevil Faulks folded his long legs and dropped to his knees. He was pointing the barrel of his gun right between the two of us, and this was fiendishly clever because the slightest turn of the wrist allowed to him to fire at first one, then the other. One is seldom kindly disposed towards a man on the point of discharging a pistol into one's body, but this man inspired feelings of a different order altogether. Observed at close range, with the attention I accorded him now, he was a bastard down to the last detail – the set of his angular features, the hard lines of his naturally twisted leer.

His nose resembled the sharp beak of a bird of prey, and his dark eyes, sunk deep beneath prominent brows, had the look of some malevolent ape. A thoroughly poisonous and dangerous creature.

"I followed you, Marjorie," he said quietly. "I suspected you were about to join this man."

His voice was deep and muffled, and so rasping that he sounded completely hoarse.

"You see, Marjorie, one had better be realistic in this life, and know when to admit defeat. You no longer love me. In fact, you have never loved me. So be it. I must accept the truth. The trouble is, I cannot accept your loving another man. And that is why I shall kill you."

Marjorie issued a quiet plea: "Nevil—"

"No, no. Don't complicate an already difficult situation.

Take a moment to collect your thoughts! I am not personally persuaded of the existence of God, but it's a theory worth considering when you're about to die."

He spoke only to her, feigning total disregard for my presence. But he kept me firmly in the corner of his eye.

"Look here, Mr Faulks," I heard myself croak. "How about we talk things over before you do something you'll regret?"

"We have nothing to say to one another."

The scene had an unreal, unbelievable quality. We were crouched in a circle on the lawn like people enjoying a picnic. Less than thirty metres away, a band was playing, and people were dancing and lovers were embracing. The comforting murmur of Princes Street rose from across the valley. And we were caught in a terrifying, chilling drama. This implacable man, crazed with jealousy, was savouring our last moments, playing the scene in slow motion, almost as if he hoped we might die of fright before he was forced to shoot. I had no strength left to speak, and knew that to do so was pointless, and dishonourable. Marjorie felt the same. She stared at me with huge, terrified eyes. She might almost have been begging *me* not to shoot.

It was seconds before I realized the wild hope in her heart. She was expecting me to try something, reproaching me for my passivity. Darling Marjorie! How right she was! No man should go to the slaughter with his head bowed, like some prize bull. People resigned to their fate are the greatest losers in life. I was not sitting on the grass, but crouched on my heels. In a single move, I could lunge forward and bring Nevil Faulks to the ground.

He would shoot, but would be unable to take aim.

I acted almost as the thought struck, as if in a trance. I needed no conscious decision; my limbs obeyed my imagination, not my will. I pounced like a leopard and my skull hit something hard, doubtless Faulks's own head. He gave a faint, rapidly stifled cry. I heard a rustle of skirts. My brow throbbed. It hurt so badly I wondered whether I had been shot. But the gold stars blurring my vision cleared, and I saw precisely what had happened. Faulks had fallen over backwards. His right arm stuck straight out, and Marjorie was kneeling on it, immobilizing the weapon as best she could. Her skirt was pulled up, and I had an electrifying vision of her white undergarments and thighs.

"The gun!" she gasped. "Quick, Jean-Marie, take it!"

Nevil made desperate efforts to free his hand, clamped tight around the revolver. Frantically, he twisted his wrist left and right.

I placed my hand on the revolver. Faulks's clenched fingers had to be prised off one by one. They snapped tight again, each time. Then I released his obstinate grip with a hard blow of my fist. He let go of the weapon. Rather than try to get it back, he rolled over onto his side and, in a single movement, clasped his left hand around Marjorie's neck.

"Jean-Marie..." she pleaded, hoarsely.

I pointed the barrel of the gun at Faulks's face, over Marjorie's shoulder. It was easy. My actions were methodical. I curled my index finger around the trigger, and the shot was fired. At point-blank range there was not much noise, which surprised me, I remember. Nevil lurched. His left hand fell away. He seemed to gather sudden strength, as if to get to his feet, but fell face forward onto the grass. A faint, hesitant trail of smoke rose from the barrel of the revolver, as if from a discarded but unextinguished cigarette. Marjorie bent over her husband and placed her hand under his cheek. When she pulled it away, her fingers were clotted with blood. She gave a shudder of disgust, and wiped her hand on the grass, over and over again.

"He's dead," she said evenly.

I had just killed a man! The ghastly silhouette of the scaffold rose before me on the lawn.

The drama had taken place on the ground, in the grass. Marjorie got to her feet and stared around her, attentively. All was perfectly calm. No one had heard anything thanks to the racket from the theatre. And we were in a small hollow, so that no one had seen anything, either. This seemed unbelievable, and yet it was the absolute truth: I had just killed a man in a public park, in bright sunshine, in the presence of a good thousand or so people. Again, I thought of the cartoon showing the hanged man in the garden square.

"Let's go, quickly," ordered Marjorie.

The revolver was still in my hand. She shook me by the wrist to release it, stowed it in her bag, then took charge of me. She glanced at the lawn as if to make sure we had left nothing behind. The grass around the corpse was clean and neat.

"We must tell the police!" I stammered, as we moved away.

She made no reply. We walked side by side along the broad path leading to the theatre. I was exhausted, as after a tremendous physical effort. I walked blindly beside her, repeating with crazed obstinacy: "I killed a man! I killed a man! I killed a man!"

13

I stared at the man posted by the turnstile. He was small, square and ape-like. Tufts of hair burst from his ears. A thick nickel watch chain was fastened to his threadbare lapel.

"Give him two pennies!" whispered Marjorie. I searched my pockets. I placed two pennies on the man's copper plate and he activated a pedal, opening the turnstile. Marjorie pushed me through. Ordinarily, I would have stepped aside to allow her through first, but I obeyed her pressure on my back and moved forward. People were scattered unevenly in the seats. We took the first row we came to and I found myself sitting next to an elderly Scotsman in a kilt. His patrician bearing and manners seemed at odds with his outlandish outfit: he wore a short, close-fitting jacket, a white frilled shirt, and a ribboned beret. A leather sporran with an engraved silver clasp hung below his waist.

I stared fixedly at the ground in front of the stage, just below the seats, where the closely packed crowd of dancers jigged. On the podium, the elderly musicians played like a collection of automata, and the music they produced was music for automata too. At the microphone, the lady in the coarse woollen skirt, with her fat calves and burgeoning chest, continued to guide the dancers' dainty entrechats with her guttural cries.

"We must go to the police, Marjorie."

I spoke very quietly, but she heard me. Without looking at me, staring straight ahead, she replied:

"No! Madness!"

"It was legitimate self-defence," I continued in the same plaintive tone, speaking out of the corner of my mouth.

"The police won't believe that."

"What are we to do?"

"Nothing. After the show, go back to your hotel. I'll telephone you this evening. What's it called?"

"The Fort William."

"Now, stop speaking to me!"

"But…"

She stood up and left, as if finding the seats uncomfortable. I saw her making her way up through the rows. She disappeared into the crowd of delighted spectators, warmly applauding the conclusion of the dance.

Never in my life had I felt so forsaken.

I could scarcely believe the appalling situation I was in. It was like a drunken man's hallucination. I felt desperately hung-over, but the effects would wear off: they couldn't possibly not wear off. There are some realities we cannot accept and must destroy by sheer force of denial.

I was sitting in an open-air theatre next to an elderly Scottish gentleman wearing a skirt, listening to dreadful music and watching couples jump up and down like idiots. And behind the theatre lay the corpse of a man I had just killed. The man's wife was watching the same show, a few metres from where I sat. My fingers smelt of cordite. Thoughts began to whirl in my head. A carousel of images – some clear, some confused. I saw Nevil's body curled on the grass. I saw Marjorie's horrified face as he attempted to strangle her. My hand could still feel the revolver's monstrous lurch as the shot was fired. When, after getting to our feet, we realized that no one had seen the dramatic incident, we had felt intense relief. And yet the absence of witnesses would be our undoing.

Now, there was only our version of events to offer to the police.

If the cops failed to accept it, we were lost. Suddenly everyone rose, like spectators at a football match when a goal is scored. I started in fright. It seemed to me that someone had brought Nevil Faulks's cadaver onto the podium; it was a while before I realized the show was over, and people were leaving. I looked all around as I left the theatre. I was certain I would see a group of police officers and nurses on the dreaded lawn, but there was no one. Faulks's corpse lay undiscovered for now.

I went back to my hotel, without seeing Marjorie. I searched for her desperately in the crowds of spectators flowing back up the paths in Princes Street Gardens. But in vain. I supposed she had left before the end of the show.

Before returning to the Fort William Hotel, I lingered on Princes Street, on the pavement overlooking the valley. From here, people could see straight down into the gardens. I could see numerous couples still sitting and lying on the lawns. Children were playing ball. Old folks chatted on the park benches. The section of the park that interested me most was hidden from view by the bulk of the open-air theatre. Down there, Nevil Faulks's bloodied body… Should we have placed the revolver in his hand, to make it look like suicide? Or taken his wallet, to suggest violent robbery?

Neither solution seemed adequate, and I understood why most killers make clumsy mistakes.

My hotel was close by. I took refuge there with some relief, but my relative sense of security was short-lived. I was impatient for Marjorie's telephone call. We needed to confer. Our salvation depended on a perfect match between our stories from now on. In essence, I represented only one half of the drama, and without the other half, I was infinitely vulnerable. The sun paled in the windows of my room, and I felt a sharp stab of nostalgia for Juan-les-Pins. The Côte d'Azur burst into life at this time of day. The noise, the nightlife, the restaurants wafting saffron and hot oil, the women, the casino.

The casino!

I remembered seeing Marjorie again across the gaming table. I wasn't gambling on red or black now. I had staked my worldly goods, my freedom, my life, on this one, straight-up bet. And if my number didn't come up...

Ivanhoe! The valiant hero had freed his lady love from her wicked tyrant lord. And what of his reward? No hearty congratulations from good King Richard, but the threat of a hempen noose.

Denise was right: heroes are the greatest fools.

There was a knock at my door. It was the hotel maid.

"Has someone telephoned for me?" I asked.

"No, sir, I wanted to know whether you would be dining here. Dinner's served soon."

"No, I'm not hungry."

"Very good, sir."

I waited for more than three hours, stretched out on the bed. Still no telephone call from Marjorie. The clink of cutlery rose from the ground floor through the open windows, followed by the squeak of the rubber-wheeled serving trolley.

Then the deep, everlasting silence of a Scottish evening.

A silence that was scarcely broken, from time to time, by the faint gurgle of taps and pipes, or the creak of a door. Then nothing. My watch showed half past ten. I could bear it no longer. I left my room and hurried down the wooden, floral-carpeted stairs.

The hotel owners and two elderly clients were watching television in a tiny room leading off the hallway. The evil, spasmodic light of the cathode ray tube hardened the strangers' features, hollowing their eye sockets with deep shadow. On the screen, a big, curly-haired fellow, rather like Danny Kaye, delivered a stream of patter whose meaning I was unable to grasp. From time to time, one of the viewers gave a ridiculous, gurgling chuckle. The old hotel proprietor, with his sad clergyman's air, noticed my presence in the door frame.

"Sit yourself down, sir!"

"No, thank you. I'm just going out for some air. Does the hotel door stay open?"

He straightened up, irritated by the interruption to his favourite pastime.

"No, sir. Will you be back late?"

"I couldn't say. I suffer from insomnia, and only a good walk..."

"I'll lend you a key," he decided, reluctantly.

And he went to fetch it from a board behind the cash register.

I had just closed the door behind me and was preparing to descend the front steps of the hotel when I heard the telephone ring. I dived back into the bright, warm hallway like a man possessed. The ringing continued, and no one seemed in any hurry to answer. I wanted to race over to where the device hung on the wall. But the proprietor of the Fort William had decided to pick it up, finally, and stared at me as he answered the call, surprised to find me standing there, motionless and expectant, when I had only just left.

"It's for you, sir."

I tore the receiver from his hands.

"Mr Valaise?"

It was a man's voice, deep and aggressive.

"Speaking."

"Mrs Marjorie has asked me to tell you that she'll be waiting for you in ten minutes at the corner of Princes Street and Frederick Street."

"Who are you?"

"A barman."

"It's Mrs Marjorie I need—"

But he had already hung up. I replaced the receiver and lingered in the doorway to the television room, watching an Indian youth perform a terrifying juggling act with daggers.

I was juggling too. Juggling with grenades.

The artiste dropped one of his blades and everyone in the room let out a cry. I left, wondering whether to take his clumsiness for a bad omen.

14

It was barely half past ten, but already people were emerging from a theatre. Life stops early in Edinburgh. The crowd of theatregoers quickly dispersed and I found myself alone in a smart, empty neighbourhood, its stone tenements rising like fortresses in the moonlight. Frederick Street stands perpendicular to Princes Street, sloping down towards the gardens. I reached the corner, but Marjorie hadn't yet arrived. I waited, leaning against the metal blind of a closed shop. The sky was as clear as a bright winter's night. No sound echoed in the still air. From time to time, a hurried figure loomed in the circles of lamplight, then melted into the darkness between. An empty bus clanked and rattled around the corner; doubtless the last of the day.

The thought of seeing Marjorie again cheered me. I felt a renewed sense of hope.

Together, maybe, we could get ourselves out of this mess. My need to hold her against me was so strong that I was no longer frightened, even by the prospect of my arrest. A few hours with her was all my heart desired! Tomorrow, in the light of day, life would do its worst, but none of that would matter, because I would have the memory of this night with Marjorie, at last.

But a distant clock chimed eleven, swiftly echoed by every clock in the city, and still Marjorie had not appeared. For the first twenty minutes, I was so certain she would come that her absence hadn't worried me. Now I was seized with sudden terror! An appalling anxiety, acute as any physical pain. A hand of steel crushed my throat. I paced back and forth, sometimes along Princes Street, sometimes along Frederick Street, then ran suddenly from one street to the next, when I thought I glimpsed a shadow or heard footsteps. There was nobody about now. In the sky, the moon's big, stupid face shone down on my distress. Marjorie was not coming. She must have been arrested in the bar, the one from which she had had me called. In fact, she had asked someone else to make the call because she was being followed. I could think of no other explanation. *There was no other explanation!* At this very moment she was sitting in front of a police officer, answering questions. I imagined her, fragile and terrified, sitting on a police station chair while gruff men tried to force her to admit she had killed her husband. The thought was intolerable, and I gave a howl of despair. Marjorie's dear face, with her freckles and her beautiful, heartbreaking eyes. The smell of Marjorie! The taste of her lips! Her timid, birdlike warmth.

"Something the matter, sir?"

I was startled to see a police officer standing motionless before me. With his black uniform and flat-topped cap, he looked like the driver of a hearse. He fixed me with a watchful eye.

"I'm waiting for someone."

"Out on the street at this time of night!"

At this time of night! I wanted to tell him about Juan-les-Pins at this time of night! Anywhere else in the world at this time of night! He was guarding a necropolis, and he didn't even know it.

I couldn't stay there. I had been waiting for over an hour, and I was under no illusion now.

"You should get along home, sir!"

He thought I'd had too much to drink. Edinburgh was full of drunks. During the day, I regularly came across characters talking to themselves, struggling to put one foot in front of the other, their eyes half closed.

"Lovely night, sir!"

"Lovely night!" I agreed, hurrying in the direction of the Royal bar.

It was a lovely night, indeed.

A lovely night to live through the blackest of nightmares.

I clung to one last hope. But the crossroads was deserted. Frederick Street marched uphill and seemed to stop somewhere in the sky. Grey, moonlit clouds scudded and collided, blown inland from the sea.

I heard a tiny noise, but it was only the wind blowing a piece of paper. What had happened to Marjorie? Had she been arrested? Or had she taken fright and fled the city? I would call at the bed and breakfast where she had been staying. But to turn up asking for her at this hour was the ultimate act of madness.

15

A marmalade cat skirted the foot of the buildings, its gait as smooth as a centipede. It spotted me and slipped away through a basement window. Its sudden disappearance heightened my sense of despair. For three or four seconds, the unknown cat had been a companionable presence.

I stood at the foot of the grand entrance to the townhouse where the Faulkses were staying. The moon was full and bright, and the ashen steps filled me with horror. The steps to the scaffold.

The black-hinged door looked more forbidding than a prison gate. I climbed the steps, telling myself I would never summon the courage to ring the bell; and rang the bell, certain I would have no idea what to say, should anyone happen to answer. The silvery chime must have been heard all along the street. The sound surprised even me, as if someone behind me had just called out my name.

Clearly, the noise had done nothing to disturb the slumbering neighbourhood, nor indeed this house. The tinkling vibrations sank into the depths of the night and silence was restored, as thick and impenetrable as before.

My nocturnal visit posed far too great a risk. I stole away like a thief caught in the act. I had reached the bottom step when a voice came out of the darkness:

"What is it you want?"

It was coming from the first floor. I looked up, terrified. The voice was not coming from Marjorie's window, but another much farther to the left. I could just make out the pale blur of a face.

"I, er… I have a message for Mrs Faulks!"

Voilà! There was no going back now. If Marjorie had been arrested, the same fate would very soon befall me.

The voice clearly belonged to the owner of the bed and breakfast. I seemed to recognize her mannered tones.

"A message for Mrs Faulks! And from whom does the message come?"

In the darkness, she had not recognized the visitor from earlier in the day (or more precisely, the day before, for it was close to one o'clock in the morning now). There was still time to seize the moment and make a run for it. But a compelling force kept me rooted to the spot. And the force was love. My thoughts came in a dizzying rush. "She's here!" I told myself. If Marjorie wasn't in the house, the old woman would have told me before quibbling over the sender of the message. We were to be reunited, at last. Calling here was madness, but I didn't care about that now.

"It's from her husband!" I called out, amazed at my own audacity.

"Oh! I see. Wait, I'll come down."

A rectangle of yellow light cut into the shadowy mass of the façade. In the window, framed like a shadow puppet, I recognized the round silhouette of the lady with the lorgnette. I kept a careful eye on Marjorie's window, hoping to discover the anxious face of my beloved behind the glass, but there was no sign of her. I waited a good five minutes before hearing the swish of slippers. Slowly, the front door opened a crack after much pulling back of bolts. A safety chain kept it from opening farther. Through the gap, I saw a portion of the elderly guest house owner. She was wearing a nightgown heavily bedecked with lace, under a blue satin housecoat that must have dated from the reign of Queen Victoria. In the heat of the moment, she had left her lorgnette on her bedside table. Without her corset, and the attendant harness work of large ladies such as herself, she looked like a sack of flour. She peered anxiously into the darkness, where I held back, as if by instinct.

"Mrs Faulks is here, is she not?"

"She's sleeping!"

O joy! I had found Marjorie. We were mere metres apart. An old lady and thirty centimetres of chain were all that lay between us.

"I must speak to her immediately."

"Oh, but I see who you are!" the old lady exclaimed. "You called here today, inquiring about a room."

"Indeed. But that's of no concern now. I have a message for Mrs Faulks, from her husband!"

"So you know him, then?"

"It was he who gave me your address," I asserted, with some aplomb.

I was prepared to blurt out anything at all. I just wanted to see Marjorie right away, and scarcely knew what I was saying.

"But how can this be?"

"A misunderstanding. I had no idea he would be in Scotland during my visit. And then we ran into one another just now, on Princes Street. And he asked me to get a message to his wife. It's most important!"

No sooner had I formed the thought than my words came tumbling out. Hempen strands for the noose that would hang me soon. Nothing mattered now.

"Please, Madame. It's of the utmost importance! *Très important!*"

My exhortations touched her heart. Awkwardly, she removed the safety chain and opened the door.

"Sit down, sir. I'll go and tell her you're here."

Two banquettes covered in purple velvet stood on opposite sides of the hall. I sat on one and watched the fat old lady climb the stairs, breathing heavily. She disappeared from view at the turn of the landing, but her increasingly laboured breathing left no doubt as to the route she had taken. She knocked at a door, softly at first, then a little louder. My blood thundered in my ears. Was Marjorie really in her room? Perhaps the owner thought she was, when in reality she had slipped out during the evening to telephone me. Some unimaginable incident had prevented her from keeping our rendezvous.

"What is it?"

A voice answered the knock. Low, fearful, sleepy. But unmistakeable. It was Marjorie.

"Forgive me, dear Mrs Faulks, but there's a gentleman here who wants to speak with you on behalf of your husband."

"One moment!"

I sensed a light tread of feet directly over my head. The door opened, and the two women began whispering. Then the owner made her way slowly downstairs once more.

"She's just coming!" she announced. "She seems very worried. I trust nothing unfortunate has happened to Mr Faulks?"

Something very unfortunate indeed had happened to Mr Faulks, but I wasn't about to enlighten her. Now was not the time. Not the time at all!

The good lady waited with me, hoping for information. She didn't dare question me herself, and was doubtless wondering how she might listen in on the conversation without appearing indiscreet.

Marjorie appeared on the half-landing. She was wearing a pale pink dressing gown knotted tight at the waist, and her hair tumbled about her shoulders. In the light of the hallway, she looked far blonder than usual. She resembled Ophelia. Clutching the balustrade, she shot me a look of complete incredulity.

"What are you doing here?" she called out. "I've had just about enough of this! Get out! Get out now or I'll call the police! And Nevil! What have you done with Nevil?"

A sleepwalker coming to his senses stark naked in the middle of the Champs-Elysées has but a pale inkling of my own astonishment at that moment. Marjorie, my beloved Marjorie, for whom I had undertaken this mad journey, for whom I had killed a man – Marjorie had become my enemy. She was staring at me now with the self-same expression as almost every inhabitant of this city: troubled and hostile.

I moved towards the stairs. The large proprietress, finding herself in my path, threw up her arms to protect her face, as if she feared I might strike her! Marjorie moved two steps back up the stairs, careful to maintain the distance between us.

"Marjorie," I begged. "My darling! Please, I beg you!"

She shrieked out loud now. And worse still, her cry sounded perfectly genuine.

"Get out of here! Mrs Morton, throw him out for the love of God! This man is mad!"

The old lady whimpered in terror. It was a frightful scene.

"Marjorie. You..."

She didn't wait for me to finish my phrase, but hurtled up the stairs. Her door slammed hard. I heard the sharp click of the key in the lock.

Dumbstruck, I stared at poor Mrs Morton as she if might offer an explanation for Marjorie's behaviour.

"Don't touch me!" she gibbered, backing up against the wall.

I nodded.

"Ridiculous," I sighed, as I left.

The marmalade cat was still at large on the deserted street when I emerged. Then it saw me, and fled to its hiding place.

16

I wandered aimlessly, but chance is an illusion where the subconscious is concerned, and I found myself yet again on Princes Street, the eternal backbone of Edinburgh. I repeated the phrase out loud as I walked: "This man is mad! This man is mad!" More than all the rest, these words had torn me apart. Marjorie had disowned me with four little words. Why this appalling change of heart? Out of cowardice? The sight of me had terrified her. Did she think I had lost my head, to come calling at Mrs Morton's? Or perhaps there was another reason. I terrified her because I was a murderer!

She had buckled, all at once, and her love for me had turned to hatred. Poor Ivanhoe! Poor hero, taken for a fool!

I was lost. Marjorie had chosen to sacrifice me. How could I be sure she would even corroborate my version of the murder? The girl on the stairs at Mrs Morton's just now would stop at nothing to keep her freedom. Denise had warned me: every man is a hero to her sort of woman. At first…

My British surroundings weighed heavily upon me. I felt like a prisoner already. And this damned transport strike prevented me from making a run for it! Oh to board a plane and be back in France. Hiding out in a little Paris hotel, or a village bistro.

I crossed the street and rested my elbows on the railings overlooking the valley. Princes Street Gardens were sunk in thick, black shadow. I could hear a faint roar, like a torrent of mud rushing at the bottom of the chasm. Would that it could drag Nevil Faulks's miserable carcass into its depths! I hated him dead just as I had hated him alive. Was his body still lying there on the lawn? Probably not. The police would be investigating his case, finding out the name of his hotel. But they would be incapable of visiting every bed and breakfast in Edinburgh in the course of a single night. News of the drama would reach Mrs Morton's with the morning papers, and not before.

Two choices presented themselves. To end it all here and now, or go to bed.

I went to bed.

I woke very early the following morning. The rain had returned, lashing my bedroom windows with renewed spite. I was soaked in sweat, and gasping for breath. The grim reality that had knocked me out cold the night before was waiting at my bedside, patient as death. I got to my feet, and swayed. My teeth were coated and rough. I plunged my head into the washbasin and treated myself to a delicious moment of icy asphyxia. Once dressed, I realized that I hadn't shaved. It was twenty past six. Heavy with rain, the grey cloud cover smothered the daylight. I decided I would shave later. My appearance mattered little. There was no one here to seduce now.

The Fort William's maid was the only other person up. She was laying the dining-room tables for breakfast. A comforting smell of coffee filled the ground floor. I asked if I might have a cup, and she brought me a full breakfast, to a table at the back of the room. Humming a tune, she buffed the gleaming skirting boards with a duster while I ate. She straightened up for a moment and looked towards me, flushed from bending over for so long.

"Lovely day!" I commented, idiotically.

She burst out laughing, and pointed to the window overlooking a wan garden flanked by high walls.

"Lovely rain!"

"Do you have the newspaper?"

"Not yet. The paper boy doesn't come before seven."

I drained my cup and headed for the door.

"Don't you have a raincoat, sir?"

"No."

"Nor an umbrella?"

"Neither."

"Would you like me to lend you one?"

An umbrella would shield my face, I decided, and make me far less conspicuous. She went to the broom cupboard and pulled a clutch of umbrellas from out of an old pot stand. Doubtless they had all been left here by former guests.

"Pick one!"

I took one at random.

Its handle was sheathed in black leather.

"Thank you. I'll return it later."

"No hurry, sir."

This was just as well, for there was every chance she would never see it again. Perhaps the cops were waiting outside until such time as they could legally arrest me?

The parked cars were all empty. The wet, grey street looked like a port town on a stormy morning. The wind gusted violently, causing passers-by to stagger sideways in alarming fashion. The bookshop on Princes Street wasn't yet open, but a man was selling newspapers in its entrance. I bought one of the Edinburgh dailies. A bold headline stretched across the page: "Strikes: No Solution." Hurriedly, I scanned the front page in search of another, more sensational story. But there was no mention of murder. And nothing in the other papers either. I bought another, just to be sure. It contained the same news as the first, and nothing more, presented in the exact same way, virtually word for word. So the corpse had not been discovered when the papers went to press. I tossed both dailies into a metal waste paper basket fixed to a lamp post.

My first day as a murderer. What was I to do? I couldn't flee. I was chained to this city by the lack of any form of transport. I couldn't join Marjorie: I was nothing but a hateful murderer in her eyes now. My inertia oppressed me. The blackened buildings suffocated me, and it seemed as if every passer-by trickling with rainwater was a policeman coming to overpower me. Thoughts of suicide gnawed at my mind, and I found the temptation hard to resist. There are times when the urge to die is as fierce as the urge to live. As implacable as a wave of slumber engulfing the mind and senses. But how to die? Even a desperate man may shrink from the act. I have always dreaded pain, because I have never truly felt it. But the imagination of it is compelling.

Then an idea came to me, and I felt a great rush of excitement, akin to real joy: I would go to the police and tell them everything. What possible good could come of wandering the streets of this miserable city, waiting for a bobbie to lay his hand on my shoulder? Yes: I would turn myself in and tell them everything. Everything! There would be no problem proving the revolver belonged to Nevil Faulks! The Scottish jury would be receptive to a plea of legitimate self-defence. On the other hand, I knew they would take a dim view of adultery. Passion, a mitigating circumstance at home in France, would be an aggravating factor here in Britain.

I crossed the main junction on Princes Street and approached the officer directing traffic. He was wearing a white raincoat, and a plastic cover over his cap.

"Could you show me where the main police station is, sir?"

The city's police headquarters were in the Old Town, across the valley. The officer was even kind enough to tell me the best bus route to take. But I was in no hurry. I intended to walk, keeping well hidden under my borrowed umbrella. I just needed to know where to go. I had all the time in the world now. The raindrops clattered on the taut silk, as loudly as on a tin roof.

The bottoms of my trousers were soaked, and my thin summer shoes were taking in water. I wandered slowly down a gently sloping path, towards the theatre. In the pouring rain, the huge stage resembled the hangar of a private flying club, discovered unexpectedly at the edge of a field. Wet bunting hung limply from the podium.

I couldn't resist taking a look at the lawn. I was powerless to do otherwise. What murderer fails to return to the scene of his crime? Morbid curiosity drove me to make the detour. I skirted the building and took the pinkish path leading to the hollow where I had killed Faulks. It all seemed as unreal as ever. It occurred to me that I had never owned an umbrella, and I felt awkward clutching the leather-bound handle. I held it tipped forward slightly in front of me, so that my field of vision extended for just a couple of metres. The proprietor of my hotel in Juan-les-Pins would have joked, in his fine, flowery accent, that "I was keeping myself waiting".

And so I was. Doubt offered some small respite: I was walking to the police station, but delaying the moment of my arrival. By the same token, I was approaching the scene of the drama, but determined to put off discovering the body – or its absence – for as long as possible.

I recognized the freshly dug flower bed, in the shape of a star. The soil was rich and dark, with a slight bluish tint. A few steps more. I stood still. I moved the umbrella aside, like a tightrope walker correcting his balance. There was the corpse, trickling with rainwater. And the revolver, wet and shining, lay at his side in the grass. I couldn't help but reach out to touch Nevil Faulks's leg. Was I hoping for some miracle? He was stiff as a log. The bullet had traversed his skull from front to back, and behind his head an appalling, dark purple mess matted his hair.

I left my umbrella upturned on the grass. The rain came in short gusts now: a filthy drizzle that plastered my face.

They say prayer can tear our thoughts from the things of this world. If so, I prayed a long while before the mortal remains of Nevil Faulks. I envied this deserted body. I recalled the phrase uttered by Roman gladiators: "We who are about to die…"

I was about to die. What jury would be so merciful as to acquit me of this murder? None, in truth. I knew that. I pictured a British courtroom, with its bewigged magistrates. They terrified me, like creatures from another planet.

They could not judge me – I was not of their kind!

A strange confrontation indeed, between the murderer and his victim, here on this expanse of lawn. The imposing castle soared overhead, with its battlements and towers, its cannons trained in scorn on the New Town, its heraldry room, its treasury, its chapels, one of which was hung with threadbare battle standards. This evening, or tomorrow, perhaps, the police would organize a reconstruction of events, but a living man would lie here, in the dead man's place. A man who, after the shot was fired, would get to his feet and return home, to one of the city's snug houses, where the light of day barely enters.

For the love of Marjorie! The phrase sounded like the title of a cheap paperback romance. With a pastel-blue cover, and fancy English-style lettering. "For the Love of Marjorie!"

Had I acted in legitimate self-defence? I tried to analyse my thoughts and deeds in the heat of the drama. Nevil was squeezing his wife's throat; strangling her. I was holding the weapon. I could have shaken Marjorie free without killing her husband. A blow to the nape of his neck with the butt of the handle would have been enough to release his grip. But no: I had quite deliberately pointed the barrel of the gun into his face. And unhesitatingly, I had pulled the trigger. This was murder, fair and square. Four or five seconds of premeditation were all it took. I was undone.

I stared around me, just as I had yesterday after firing the shot. Like yesterday, Princes Street Gardens were quiet. In the distance, very far off, I saw two gardeners busying themselves around a flower bed. A third was pushing a motorized mower, its sputterings echoing across the valley. A pair of lovers were walking near the floral clock – office workers, no doubt, stealing their fill of kisses and heated declarations in this discreet spot, before heading off to work. I picked up my umbrella and walked away.

"What sort of spade, sir?"

I hadn't chosen one yet, and shrugged evasively.

The ironmonger, an old man with a bald head and purple nose, considered me through an antique monocle.

"For what purpose is it, sir?"

I could hardly tell him I would be using it to bury a gentleman in a flower bed in Princes Street Gardens.

"Camping," I replied.

"I see!"

He went to fetch two spades from a rack. Solid tools crafted in thick metal, with a short shaft ending in a triangular handle. They differed in size only. I chose the smaller of the two and he made me a fine parcel, all wrapped in corrugated cardboard. It was an insane plan, but since the beginning of this whole business I had followed the path of madness at every turn. Standing in rapt contemplation of Nevil Faulks's corpse, I had decided that if I could delay the discovery of the body for another forty-eight hours, I could perhaps get back to France despite the strike. A far-fetched itinerary took shape in my mind: I would hitch-hike to a port on the west coast, and charter a fishing boat to take me to Ireland. There would be no strike there and I could catch a train to Shannon, the international airport, a stopover for long-haul transatlantic flights. Forty-eight hours' respite. Perhaps not even that... Thirty hours would do it. Rather than hitch-hike, I could buy a motorcycle. Safer. How long would it take to reach Glasgow?

Emerging from the ironmonger's store I was surprised to see the weather had turned almost fine. The sky had cleared and rays of sunshine threaded the few, friendly-looking clouds. The streets were suddenly filled with people.

Nearing the cadaver, my blood turned to ice. A young mother and her little daughter of three or four were approaching, chatting happily. The child held its mother's hand and paused from time to time to gather daisies from the edge of the lawn. The woman wore a grey raincoat with epaulettes, and her red hair shone through a transparent rain cap.

She would see the body. She couldn't fail to see it. I crouched down beside Nevil.

"Shouldn't be lying in the damp grass like that, old man! That's a short cut to rheumatism, that is."

I laughed – a poor, thin laugh with less cheer than the creak of a rusty weather vane. The woman and child passed by. They stared at the corpse.

"Why's that man lying down?" asked the little girl.

"I expect he's tired, Sally. He's been running!"

They moved along at a snail's pace. I feared the woman would have second thoughts and come back to take a closer look at the man lying flat on his stomach in the wet grass. But she had forgotten him already, too distracted by her little girl. When they had gone, I set to work. There was nothing complicated about it. I simply had to make a big enough hole in the soil that had been dug over for the flower bed. Big enough to take Nevil Faulks's body. I worked furtively, digging with the frenzied haste of a fox terrier. The wet soil clung to the spade. I created a sort of ditch, piling the earth to either side. Every twenty seconds I stopped work to look around me. The gardens were beginning to fill with crowds of idlers.

An elderly couple approached, carrying two folding chairs. They settled on the lawn about twenty metres from me, and set out their picnic. The sun made a swift, sudden appearance, radiant between two clouds. The damp lawns glistened. I opened my umbrella and placed it above Nevil's shattered head, so that he looked like someone stretched out asleep. What was Marjorie doing, all this time?

Was she waiting it out, or had she lost her nerve and told everything to the police? What I was doing now would lead to my inevitable conviction. To bury a body was a wicked act indeed. After this, how could anyone accept that I had killed this man in self-defence?

The elderly couple had a dog on a lead. A vile, white mutt with black patches. Once they were settled, the man let the dog run free. After a few circuits of the lawn, the dog trotted over to the corpse, barking. It had a wall eye and was truly one of the vilest mutts that ever lived. The woman shouted herself hoarse, calling him back, but the dog was having none of it. In vain, I tried to push him away with my toe.

Seeing his wife's lack of success, the man brought himself over. He was small, with sparse teeth and the look of a retired gentleman's valet. His chin and nose made close acquaintance. He brandished the lead with a threatening air, but the animal was completely unmoved.

"Here, Pudding! Have you quite finished?"

He seized the dog by the collar. The catch clicked shut and he dragged the frightful mutt away. The dog's hind leg kicked at the handle of the umbrella. The fragile silk canopy rolled over, almost completely uncovering Faulks. It was an appalling moment. The old chap was struck by my friend's odd position and absolute stillness.

"Is he ill?" he asked.

I found the strength to smile, with a knowing wink.

"A drop too much of the whisky! We were drinking all night at my place, and I wanted him to get some air before going back to his wife. She's not a very accommodating woman."

"But he's fast asleep!"

The old man drew back his lips, revealing his white, empty gums.

"You should cover him over. It's not wise to lie there, in the wet grass."

He moved away, dragging the now silent dog. I was terrified he would bend down and see the hideous wound frothing at the back of Nevil's neck. I feared he would look to his right and see my camping spade planted in the earth, in the flower bed. Above all, I was afraid he would notice my stricken expression. Fortunately, he was very elderly indeed. He had eyes for no one but the frightful Pudding, and his lady wife.

The hole was big enough. But how to drag the body into it without being seen by the little old couple? I would have to wait until they left. Sitting cross-legged just a few centimetres from the dead man, I chewed some blades of grass to calm my febrile state. From time to time, I pushed Faulks with my foot, moving him slightly so that my neighbours on the lawn would think he had shifted in his sleep. Two interminable hours passed in this way. I could feel myself taking leave of my senses. The sun seemed to ricochet slowly among the clouds. It disappeared, then returned, then sank from view again almost immediately. The lawn brightened and darkened. The umbrella cast a crooked, dark circle over Faulks's torso, and the shadow faded, then reformed. I began to feel sleepy. I forgot where I was or what I was doing there. I wanted to nod off. I was about to close my eyes when reality gave me a violent poke and I started awake like a man who dreams he is falling into the abyss.

"Will you be quiet, Pudding!"

I looked in their direction. They were leaving. The dog was barking again, but cheerfully now. The old lady was clutching the lead while the man folded the chairs and slipped his arm underneath their backrests, to carry them home.

Their slow gestures and monotonous, nasal tones were more unbearable to me than the wait that had preceded their departure.

They went on their way. Before disappearing from view, the man looked back and gave me a parting nod of the head.

17

The hole was scarcely deep enough, and an oblong mound lay across the flower bed once I had covered Faulks's body with earth. I levelled the soil as best I could. Then I walked all around the flower bed, examining it from every angle. There was nothing suspicious-seeming, and the bump that had bothered me at first looked deliberate now. Reassured, I wrapped the spade back up in its corrugated cardboard, and wondered where to dump it.

Princes Street Gardens would be too risky. A bottle top would look out of place on these immaculately trimmed lawns. The discovery of a spade clearly destined for heavier duties than ornamental gardening might alarm the park keepers and – who knows? – lead to the discovery of the secret grave.

I left the hated lawn, my umbrella under one arm and my spade under the other. The grass was flattened slightly where I had dragged the body, but the next burst of rain – which seemed imminent – would restore it. My shoes and trouser bottoms were covered in mud. I cleaned them as best I could before making my way back up to Princes Street. But I was eager to take a bath and change.

On returning to the Fort William Hotel, I was surprised to find myself thinking about Marjorie without sorrow or regret. The vile chore I had just accomplished had cured me of her utterly. In truth, my ardour had cooled the day after her departure from Juan-les-Pins, only to be rekindled by her letter. It was a kind of bewitchment. Away from her, my sanity was restored.

In the quiet street, the hotel's gold lettering, painted on the fanlight, was all that distinguished it from the other buildings. Its discretion was reassuring. Climbing the steps, I wondered if I might snatch a few hours of sleep before continuing my adventure, for I was dead with fatigue. But I was becoming careless. I had to act. If I indulged myself now, I would end up waiting for the strike to be over, before leaving.

The maid was washing the stone-flagged lobby floor with a bucket of water. She was kneeling, and her meagre goat's backside pointed miserably skyward. She turned her head as I came in, and delivered an unfriendly stare.

"Here's your umbrella, miss. Thank you – it was most useful."

She made no reply, but stayed kneeling with her hands pressed flat on the soapy floor cloth. I added:

"Where should I leave it?"

"If you wouldn't mind giving it to me, sir?"

I looked in the direction of the new voice. What I saw stung me like two sharp slaps to the face. A man of average height had just appeared in the sitting-room doorway. He wore a black raincoat and held a felt hat by the tips of his fingers.

"This way, please," he said, standing back to let me into the small room, dominated by the television set on its stand.

I stepped inside.

"Inspector Brett!"

I nodded dully, as if Inspector Brett was a lifelong acquaintance.

The hotel proprietor was already in the room. He had been keeping the inspector company, providing as much as detail about me as he was able.

He fixed me with a scowl of such fierce disapproval it was almost comical. The poor man looked like a bad-tempered dog straining at the leash.

"You are Jean-Marie Valaise?" (He pronounced my name John Merry Vel-eyes).

"Indeed, why do you ask?"

The strangest thing was that the inspector had managed to relieve me of my umbrella, and hook it over his own arm.

"I'm very sorry to trouble you, Mr Valaise, but I'm afraid I must ask you to accompany me to the police station."

I knew the form. And told myself this was it. As a student, I had sat the entrance exam to a prestigious school of engineering, and failed. I saw myself now, poring over the typed list of successful candidates. I couldn't find my name, which should have been somewhere near the bottom, under "V". "This is it," I had thought to myself, and I had savoured the moment. Failure is heady stuff. Less so than victory, perhaps, but its reach is deeper by far.

"What's this about?"

"I'd like to take a statement from you, regarding a certain matter."

"Can't you take it here?"

"That would be difficult, sir."

He radiated the calm obstinacy so characteristic of his profession. He had a prominent, bald, pink forehead, a cherry-tipped nose, red cheekbones and expressionless but obdurate features.

"And if I refuse to accompany you?" I asked, irascibly.

He showed no sign of anger, but removed a sheet of grey paper from his pocket.

"I have a summons, sir. My apologies for not presenting it straight away."

"In that case, I'll come with you."

"That seems the reasonable thing to do, sir."

"May I shave first?"

It had just occurred to me that I was still carrying the muddy spade wrapped in cardboard under my arm. If I was granted permission to clean up, I might find a way to get rid of it. I regretted not hurling it into a drain, or even leaving it in a waste bin somewhere in town.

"I should like to get this over with as quickly as possible, sir. I don't expect it'll take us long."

He was polite but firm. I had nothing to gain by insisting.

"In that case, let's go."

We passed through the door of the little sitting room, back out into the hall. The inspector stopped in surprise. I could see what had caught his eye: my muddy footprints on the stone flags. The maid was still scrubbing the floor. She hadn't noticed the mess I had made, spoiling her work. The inspector's gaze halted for a brief second, then followed the footprints. He reached my mud-covered shoes and sniffed once or twice, saying nothing. Then he continued along the hall to the front door, taking big strides so as not to tread in the wet. I thought, desperately, "I have to get shot of this blasted spade."

But how?

By leaving it in the hall? The proprietor would find it and take it straight to Inspector Brett.

I was outside now, standing beside the inspector with my hastily wrapped package under my arm. He still had hold of my umbrella. A reflex, surely? People were born carrying an umbrella in this country. The inspector must have forgotten it was not his.

A big, black Jaguar topped with a blue light was parked in a neighbouring street. I was struck by this detail. Brett had chosen to park the police car here, despite the ample space in front of the hotel, to avoid attracting my attention. He clearly believed I would make a run for it at the sight of the car. And if he believed that, then he believed me guilty of a serious crime.

A uniformed officer waited, leaning against the bonnet. He returned to the driver's seat as we approached, and strapped a safety belt across his chest.

Brett opened one of the rear doors. I pretended to stumble as I stepped off the kerb, and kicked my compromising package under the car. I took my seat with a relaxed air, and even allowed myself the luxury of greeting the driver. He didn't respond, but waited for Brett to take his seat.

The Inspector dropped into the seat beside me with a satisfied sigh. He held the camping spade across his knees.

18

The police headquarters building was at least four hundred years old and probably listed as a historic monument. The façade was quite beautiful. Before crossing the threshold, I admired its mullioned windows and carved cornice.

The interior was a disappointment. The building had been gutted and fitted with large, very bright modern offices and an abundance of chrome and Formica. Inspector Brett invited me to take a seat, and removed his raincoat. Under it he wore a sad, rather crumpled brown suit with broad lapels curling slightly at the tips. He hung his raincoat and old felt hat on the coat stand then, after a moment's hesitation, placed the umbrella and spade on his desk, as if he already considered them to be pieces of evidence. On our journey to the station he had patted and squeezed the parcel continually as if trying to guess its contents.

Eventually, the cardboard had split next to the blade, and the inspector had got mud on his fingers.

He sat down. A folder lay open on his green desk blotter. It contained a single sheet of paper on which someone had scribbled a few notes. Brett ran through them before speaking.

"Do you know Mrs Marjorie Faulks, sir?"

"I do."

"And Nevil Faulks, her husband?"

"I've not had the honour."

I detected a quiet sound, like the nibbling of a mouse. I saw a small microphone trained on me, on the desktop. Brett had just switched on a tape recorder. He saw I had noticed the mic and, for the first time since our meeting, he gave a slight smile.

"Ah! Yes, I must warn you that anything you say will be taken down and may be used in evidence against you. Your name is Jean-Marie Valaise, is it not?"

"You've already asked me that, and my answer was 'Yes'."

"You live in Paris?"

"Number 26 rue des Plantes!"

"Profession?"

"Sales representative, for adding machines."

"How long have you known Mrs Faulks?"

I closed my eyes. I felt as if Marjorie had filled my whole existence for years.

"I met her last week, in Juan-les-Pins."

"Under what circumstances?"

"She got into the wrong car, and was sitting in mine by mistake."

"And you saw her again after that?"

"At the casino, by pure chance."

"And then?"

"She had left her beach bag in my car – she came to my hotel to fetch it."

"And then?"

"And then that's all! Why all these questions, Inspector?"

Thanks to the microphone, I felt I was addressing an invisible audience rather than one police officer. I was caught in the midst of a great, ghostly circle.

"Mrs Faulks has lodged a complaint against you, Mr Valaise."

"What!"

"She claims that you have followed her persistently since that meeting on the Côte d'Azur. You have disrupted her marriage. You have even issued threats against her husband."

A new Marjorie altogether stood before me now: treacherous and calculating. A thorough-going bitch! She had decided to place the blame for her husband's murder squarely on me. Her Machiavellian plan left me feeling quite sick; I was too weak even to bear her any ill will. I thought of the beach in Juan-les-Pins, of Denise, of meals in the restaurant with its wooden deck that smelt like a floating lido, of my hot hotel room overlooking the garage.

I had given up all that for an idiotic dream. I had lost everything, believing myself in love with that half-crazed girl.

I had made no reply. Brett persisted:

"So, what do you say?"

"It's a lie."

"In that case, why write her this love letter?"

He removed a sheet of typed paper from a drawer in his desk and explained:

"This is the English translation of your letter. The original is at our laboratory, as I speak."

They had had a busy morning. Almost as busy as mine!

"It's true I was in love with Mrs Faulks, but I deny persistently following her, Inspector."

"Do you deny calling at her lodgings last night, at around one o'clock?"

"No, but—"

"You told the proprietor that Mr Faulks had asked you to give his wife a message, did you not?"

"That was a ruse, so that she would let me in."

"Why did you want to be let in at that hour?"

I had no idea what to say. Why put up a fight? I was sinking fast.

"You knew that Mr Faulks was not at Mrs Morton's lodging house?"

"No, not at all!"

"And yet you claimed you had come with a message from him."

He observed me impassively, and I stared at the red hairs on the backs of his big hands, placed flat on the folder. He lacked that alert, cat-like expression so often attributed to police officers. Doubtless he was a conscientious man who accomplished his work without passion, his chief weapon being his implacably logical mind.

I cleared my throat.

"I didn't know that Mr Faulks had come to Edinburgh with his wife."

"Indeed?"

"I had no idea."

"And yet Mrs Faulks claims that you approached her while she was out walking with her husband."

"She's lying."

"Why would she be lying?"

"I have no idea, but she's lying!"

"Why would she have lodged a complaint against you?"

"I should like to know."

"You never saw the Faulkses together?"

"No."

"You did not arrange to meet Mr Faulks at the corner of Frederick Street and Princes Street at around 11 p.m.?"

I was dumbstruck now. Up to this point, Marjorie's treachery had followed a certain logic. I understood her plan perfectly: to make me look like a crazed tormentor. Clearly, she believed that by reporting me to the police she was covering herself and heaping all the blame on my head. But why the devil was she complicating things with this ridiculous story about a meeting arranged long after Nevil had been murdered? The whole thing was beyond my comprehension, and it bothered me quite as much as the still unformulated accusation hanging over me.

"I never arranged to meet Mr Faulks."

"In that case, what *were* you doing last night, on the corner of Princes Street and Frederick Street?"

"I was waiting for Mrs Faulks. She was the one who arranged the meeting. She didn't come, and that's why I went around to her lodgings. I was worried."

"When did she contact you to arrange the meeting?"

"She asked a barman to call me. At twenty to eleven."

"According to her landlady, Mrs Faulks stayed in her room all evening."

"Listen here, Inspector, it seems to me that Mrs Faulks is a scheming bitch and Mrs Morton is a mad old woman."

"You're making a very serious accusation, Mr Valaise. Mrs Morton is the widow of Colonel Morton, who served with great distinction in the last war."

"A person can be a colonel's widow and still be stark, staring mad!" I thundered, angrily. "I've had enough of this, Inspector! Marjorie Faulks claims I've been pestering her, does she? She wants to pass me off as an obsessive lunatic? I'll prove to you I'm not. Can you read French?"

"Very badly!"

"Well, get your translators to translate this, written in Marjorie's own hand. I received it four days ago in Juan-les-Pins."

I produced my wallet and took out the passionate letter that had prompted my journey to Scotland.

I congratulated myself on having kept it. I would thwart the bitch's plan now.

The inspector seized the sheet of paper. Then he pressed a button on his intercom.

"Ask Morrow to come in, will you?" he said quietly.

A moment later, a tall, thin devil with an appalling squint entered the room. Brett held the letter out to him and asked him to translate it. The new arrival spoke perfect French: he translated the letter almost instantly. The inspector listened, resting his chin on one of his large hands. It was impossible to read his thoughts; he maintained a doggedly impassive expression, with even a touch of polite boredom, as when friends ask their small son to entertain on the piano. When the reading was finished, Brett took my letter and slipped it into his folder.

"I'll return it to you later, Mr Valaise. Do you have the envelope?"

"No, I threw it away."

He sniffed, then turned to his colleague.

"Thank you, Morrow, that'll be all for now."

We were alone again. Alone with the microphone, capturing and betraying my every sigh.

"I'm going to ask you to wait a moment in the next room, sir. If you'd like anything to eat, just ask my men."

He pressed the intercom again and delivered his instructions. A uniformed officer entered the room.

"This way, sir."

I was following obediently, when Brett's voice rang out.

"Oh! Mr Valaise, one more thing…"

He had just torn open the cardboard wrapping around the spade. Lying across his desk, the object took on an appalling significance.

"Would it be indiscreet of me to ask why you carry a muddy spade with you when walking about town?"

"I found it."

It was a terrible answer, and I was ashamed at how pathetic it made me seem.

With a small jerk of the head, Brett instructed the officer to take me away.

The next room was much smaller than the inspector's office. It was furnished with two tables and a row of steel-framed chairs, like the seating in a cheap cafeteria. Two telephones and a typewriter stood on one table. On the other lay a pile of technical magazines about the British motor industry. The officer told me to sit down and asked if I wanted anything to eat or drink. I said I didn't. At this, he sat down at the typewriter, excused himself and continued typing a great many copies of a text written very small on sheets of flimsy paper. He was young, and applied himself to his task.

I leafed through the magazines. I didn't feel like reading in English, and stared instead at the photographs of cars. The magazines were already out of date, and the vehicles they featured looked old-fashioned.

The door opened and Brett walked through, holding the spade in one hand. He smiled as he crossed to the opposite door. Just before leaving the room, he turned.

"Oh! Mr Valaise, did I mention that Nevil Faulks failed to return to his lodgings last night?"

19

Since arriving in Scotland, I had spent my time waiting. To me, Edinburgh was a drab purgatory where I must expiate my sins by waiting for a bell to ring, or someone to arrive. The hours piled up around me. I persisted in hoping life would return to its normal pace, but still it stagnated, and I sank like a man caught in a stinking swamp. I have no idea how long I sat at the table with the dog-eared magazines full of all the despondent solemnity of the British Isles. They even smelt of Britain. I was aware of the comings and goings in Brett's room; and in the corridor, the sound of voices and telephones. There was the drone of traffic outside too, and the heavy clank of buses. My guard didn't seem to have been ordered to keep constant watch on me. Often, he stepped out of the room, leaving me alone. At one point, he disappeared into Brett's office and returned with a spool of tape. He threaded the spool onto his own machine. It contained my interview with the inspector. The officer used a foot pedal to start and stop the reel, phrase by phrase. His fingers flew as he typed our conversation on his brand-new typewriter, but he showed no interest in what he was transcribing. I even wondered whether he was aware that I was one half of the dialogue.

After working hard for a time, he allowed himself a cigarette, and offered one to me. I refused. Was I a detainee, or merely a witness? How would he react if I got to my feet and declared

I was going back to my hotel? I decided to try my luck, and asked the whereabouts of the toilets.

"In the corridor, sir. The door at the end."

He went back to hammering at his Underwood. I left the room, unaccountably thrilled by this semblance of freedom. But as I emerged into the corridor, an alarm rang and an officer appeared. He sat himself on the leather banquette without looking at me. There were thick bars on the toilet window. When I returned to the secretary's office I was surprised to hear my own voice.

"Listen here, Inspector, it seems to me that Mrs Faulks is a scheming bitch and Mrs Morton is a mad old woman…"

The officer looked up distractedly. I was of no interest to him. A moment later, I was visited by a preoccupied-looking man in a white coat. He held a lidless cardboard box in one hand and a metal spatula in the other.

"Allow me, sir?"

He knelt down in front of me and lifted one of my feet. Then he placed the empty box under the sole of my shoe and scraped the latter with his spatula. The mud plastering my shoes was drying now, and fell easily into the cardboard box with a noise like a sudden rain shower. The man in the white coat might have been fitting me for a pair of brogues.

"Thank you, sir."

More time passed, and I was about to ask for some food, but found I had no desire to eat a meal in this police station. To do so would be an abdication of hope.

And so I fell asleep, leaning back in my chair with my head resting against the partition wall.

The young officer was still typing. And my voice came in

snatches from the tape recorder, a strange voice, tinged with the accents of fear. I barely recognized it as my own.

"Mr Valaise, if you please!"

I started. My elbow had slipped and I almost fell out of my chair. Brett was standing in front of me. No doubt he had just eaten lunch; his face was quite flushed.

"Come into my office, would you?"

Why did I feel the need to ask the time? It seemed the most important thing in the world to me.

"It's two o'clock in the afternoon, sir."

He must have taken my question as some sort of reproach, because he added:

"Forgive me for keeping you waiting so long. There were a few essential checks to carry out, as I'm sure you understand?"

"What checks?"

"That's what we're going to talk about now. Do you need anything?"

"Yes, a glass of water."

My short sleep had left me feeling dreadfully hung-over.

"Are you sure you wouldn't like a glass of beer?"

What was I to make of all this solicitous attention? Was my case resolved?

"I'd prefer water, Inspector."

His office contained a cupboard, divided into two sections. The first was fitted with a coat rail, the second contained a small sink. He took a glass from a narrow shelf and rinsed it carefully before handing it to me, filled to the brim. The water tasted faintly of chlorine, like all city water. Brett brandished Marjorie's letter as I drank.

"I requested a graphologist's report on this letter, Mr Valaise. I'm sorry to have to tell you that it was not written by Mrs Faulks."

I stared at him, trying to ascertain if this was a trap. Then I drained my glass of water. This new mystery was completely beyond me.

"What do you say to that?"

I needed to think. Every mystery is an illusion, like luck. Apply reason, and you'll find a way through.

"How did you acquire a specimen of her handwriting?"

"Dear Lord, by the simplest means possible: by asking her to write a few lines on a piece of paper!"

The paper in question was in his folder. Obligingly, he held it out to me, with the letter.

"See here. I even asked her to write the same text. The translator claims that the message written by Mrs Faulks under our noses is full of mistakes. She writes your language very, very badly. As for the characters, you can see they have nothing in common with those in the first letter."

"She's disguised her handwriting!"

"No, Monsieur."

He spoke the French word in so appalling an accent I found it hard to suppress a smile.

"The expert is quite positive: *the two letters were not written by the same person, and the first was definitely written by a man*!"

He took back the two documents and placed them in his folder. Brett's attitude had changed. No longer the cautious, neutral officer of that morning, he was a determined man now, certain of his facts.

"There is still no sign of Nevil Faulks, Mr Valaise."

"What can I do about that?"

"The analysis of the mud on your shoes shows that it's the same as that clinging to the shovel you say you… found. And so, where did you… find it exactly?"

I gave no reply.

"In an ironmonger's shop on Charlotte Street, am I right?"

He rose and lifted an umbrella from the coat stand. It was the one lent me by the maid at the Fort William Hotel.

"We found traces of dried blood on the underside of the silk," Brett continued. The laboratory will carry out a more complete analysis, but our chemists are already convinced that it's human."

He laid the umbrella across his desktop, its steel tip pointing straight at me.

"Would you show me your hands, Mr Valaise?"

Miserably, I held them out in front of me. At nursery school, a large, severe teacher would inspect our hands every morning. I held mine out now with the same frightened gesture, one I hadn't performed for at least twenty-five years! And Brett did exactly what the schoolmistress had done before: turned my hands over with a slight twist of the wrist.

"You've no scratches, sir. How did blood come to be on this item? It's fresh blood, yet the umbrella spent several months in a cupboard before it was lent to you." I couldn't help but admire his technique. He was working his way through the investigation like a labourer scything a hay field. Obstructions fell at his approach, and the truth was laid bare, as clean-cut as the lawns in Princes Street Gardens.

"You have very fine hands, Mr Valaise. Are they the hands of a murderer?"

I let them fall at my sides, exhausted and overwhelmed.

"Yes," I sighed, "they are."

20

I was sitting in the chair facing Brett. The tape recorder emitted its quiet electric buzz. The sound terrified me whenever I paused in my confession, forcing me to continue. I began at the beginning, the moment when, while lunching in a restaurant in Juan-les-Pins, I spotted a woman sitting in my car. I told him about the meeting at the casino, the beach bag she came to fetch from my hotel. I told him about the frenzied state in which I had written my letter. I talked about Denise, and our few carefree days together.

"I don't know the Côte d'Azur at all," said Brett, with a melancholy air.

I was touched by his words. But he quickly recovered his gruff concentration. I think he too was a little frightened of the tape recorder. He let slip nothing but the occasional, thoroughly professional, phrase. When I came to Marjorie's letter, quite without thinking, I seized the inspector's arm. He had to believe me.

"She wrote it, Inspector. I swear it was her! Your expert's made a mistake, or perhaps… No, wait, I see it now – she was frightened of her jealous husband. What if she had the letter copied out by a friend, as a precautionary measure?"

Brett made no reply. He stroked his close-shaven, pink cheeks, offset now, after lunch, by a network of delicate purple veins.

"You don't believe me?"

"Go on, Mr Valaise."

I went on: the telegram, my arrival in Edinburgh, my stupefaction at finding no one at the Learmonth, my searches, Mrs Morton's bed and breakfast, my wait at the street corner, and...

"Dear God, Inspector! I will prove to you that Marjorie felt exactly as I did!"

I began a vigorous search of my pockets, and found what I was looking for: a small, balled-up piece of paper. I smoothed it out between my thumb and forefinger while translating the text for Brett.

> Dear Jean-Marie,
>
> Thank you, thank you, thank you.
>
> Thank you for being here. Alas, I'm with my husband. I'll explain. Be in Princes Street Gardens near the bandstand this evening at 5.
>
> *Je vous aime.*
>
> "Your *Ma Jolie*".

"She dropped this note in front of me when she walked by, on her husband's arm."

Brett took the letter and opened the folder containing the handwriting specimens.

"This was not written by Mrs Faulks," he said.

I felt my insides heave, as if with an irresistible urge to vomit. There was clearly some confusion over the graphologists' reports. Try as I might, turning the problem every which way, I could see no other explanation.

Still perfectly calm, perfectly precise, Brett said quietly, "Go on, Mr Valaise."

*

When my confession was complete, the inspector stopped the tape recorder.

"Thank you. You are now under arrest!"

Guards came to fetch me. They escorted me down endless corridors. A veritable labyrinth, from which I was sure the execution chamber was the only way out.

I was locked into a space that looked nothing like a cell, or nothing like my idea of a cell, at least. It was a proper bedroom, plain and simple, with a white wooden bedstead, washbasin and commode. True, the window was barred, but the panes weren't frosted. It looked out onto a narrow, sloping street at the bottom of which there rose an immense, black building. People were going quietly about their business. I could see a bric-a-brac shop window, in the centre of which was a huge, red-bellied set of bagpipes. From a distance, the instrument looked like a new-born calf on spindly legs. A guard served me a meal on a tray: poached haddock and a slice of veal with undercooked potatoes. As a gesture to this Frenchman, no doubt, someone had added a basket full of bread rolls. Everything had the sad taste of fried food gone cold, the authentic flavour of Scottish cuisine. I ate little. Besides, I wasn't hungry. When I had finished I banged on the door. The sight of the leftover food made me feel sick. But no one came. And so I stretched out on the bed to think. Closing my eyes, I felt I was still in Juan-les-Pins.

I would have given what little clearly remained of my life to experience the heady smells and sounds of the Côte one more time…

They came to fetch the tray. There were two of them.

Were they suddenly afraid I might try to escape? The idea would certainly never have crossed my mind. The prospect of wandering the hostile streets of Edinburgh terrified me more than prison. Here, at least, there was nothing left to decide. I would let events unfold, hands laced behind my head. It was up to others to act now. Up to others to make sense of it all. I was letting go. I had committed an act of madness, and I was preparing to pay the price. The secret of life, the one great secret, is acceptance. A man who accepts his fate is a happy man indeed! The two guards left, but just as they were closing the door, a third came to escort me to Brett's office.

The inspector was smoking a black pipe. He looked up as I was shown in, and quickly placed it in an ashtray, as if ashamed to be found smoking in front of the accused.

He was looking at me strangely.

"Have you found the body?" I asked, taking my seat.

I was beginning to feel at home in the office. I was familiar with the chair's straight back and slanting armrests. I savoured the aroma of light tobacco. Quietly, the pipe fizzled out.

"One moment, please."

Brett fixed a new reel into the tape recorder. The motor began its feeble hum, thrumming *ad nauseam*.

"We have exhumed Nevil Faulks, indeed." He hesitated to continue; doubtless he had a delicate question to ask, and was wondering how best to broach it.

"Mr Valaise..."

I appreciated his courtesy. In France, no policeman would address a murderer as "Monsieur".

"Mr Valaise, there is something not right about your confession. You claim to have killed Nevil Faulks shortly after five o'clock in the afternoon, do you not?"

"And I'll reaffirm it now, it's the truth!"

"No!"

"I swear—"

"You'll swear to nothing!"

He looked angry now. His admirable patience had deserted him.

"Faulks was killed between 11 p.m. and midnight. The forensic examiner is positive!"

"Dear God," I stammered, "he lay dying for six hours! And we thought he was dead."

"He was killed outright – the bullet went straight through his brain. You claim legitimate self-defence and seek to implicate Mrs Faulks in the crime, but it won't work, Mr Valaise. Because you'll be forced to alter the stated time of the murder to support your theory. Unfortunately for you, Nevil Faulks dined with his wife in a restaurant on Aberdeen Street at 7 p.m. After that, he went back to Mrs Morton's, still in the company of his wife. At around 10 p.m. he received a telephone call from you. Mrs Morton took the call and put you through to the Faulkses' room. She's quite certain of that: the caller had a French accent! A little later, Nevil Faulks called to tell you he was on his way to your agreed meeting, and he left."

I was suddenly alone, in a fourth dimension. Brett was convinced he was walking on solid ground, but I knew he was treading on smoke. And opium smoke at that! I knew the truth all right; but as the result of I knew not what skulduggery, it no longer looked like the truth.

Everyone was lying to save Marjorie.

"It's impossible, Inspector. Impossible! I killed him at 5 p.m.!"

His anger gave way to pity.

"You're denying a bundle of evidence. Your technique might persuade a French jury, Mr Valaise, but it's not the sort of thing to dent the quiet assurance of their Scottish counterparts, believe me!"

I clasped my hands until my knuckles were purple. I could see why people banged their heads against walls. I felt a burning desire to break my head open and roll on the floor.

"Inspector, either I'm stark, staring mad, or Marjorie Faulks has several accomplices, keeping her out of all this."

Brett turned white, and his network of tiny veins faded to blue.

"I don't believe you're mad, Mr Valaise. But I believe it would suit you to pass yourself off as such. Between 5 and 6 p.m., Nevil Faulks was in a meeting with three highly respectable gentlemen in the offices of a large building firm. At the restaurant in Aberdeen Street, before dinner, he enjoyed a cocktail at the bar with his wife. The barman, the head waiter and a waitress all formally identified the body, half an hour ago! Mrs Morton too! Are you seriously suggesting that these people are all lying to save Mrs Faulks?"

I felt I was running blindfold towards the parapet of a high roof. Perhaps I was mad? Madness is a form of delusion, after all.

The inspector recovered his composure. Nervously, he picked up his pipe, sucked at it once or twice then put it back down on his desk after hesitating to relight it.

"Last night, a police officer spoke to you on the corner of Princes Street and Frederick Street. You claimed to be waiting for a friend."

"I was waiting for Mrs Faulks."

He laughed out loud. A short, angry, insulting laugh, like a snap from a bad-tempered dog.

"And when she didn't come, you simply went around to her lodgings! A rather illogical thing to do, wouldn't you say?"

A pause. The tape turned in the emptiness. I pictured the secretary in the neighbouring office. He would get a decent moment's respite. He might wonder whether the interview was over.

"Your crime was premeditated, Mr Valaise."

"No!"

"Oh, but it was. The revolver that killed Faulks was French."

Another low blow, leaving me thoroughly winded.

"Well?" Brett insisted.

"Do you know what, Mr Brett? At times like this, a man ought to be able to wake himself up!"

"Is that all you can say?"

"That's all, Inspector. I killed Nevil Faulks; but I killed him at five in the afternoon, in the presence of his wife, in order to save her from him."

He heaved a sigh.

"So that half a dozen people who saw him and spoke to him at that precise moment, and subsequently, are the victims of a collective hallucination?"

"They may be mistaken."

"A doppelganger, then. Or, who knows, an identical twin brother? Come on now, Mr Valaise, I thought you Frenchmen had a more logical cast of mind!"

"I killed Faulks at about five o'clock, give or take a minute or two."

"And the body remained on the lawn?"

"Yes."

"Mr Valaise, I'm afraid you're going to have to come up with another story. Yesterday evening, the park keepers mowed the lawns in Princes Street Gardens. All of the lawns, as they do every evening. If they had found a body, I think they might have told us!"

21

In my student days, a classmate who was well connected in the world of cinema arranged for me to be an extra in a film. The scene in which I "featured" was a trial scene. I was a member of the public. The director asked us all to look engrossed by staring at a small light bulb above the camera. I found it very hard not to stare into the camera; I feared my mental effort would be obvious on the screen. But when the film was finished, I appeared for a just a few fractions of a second, and my face attracted no more attention than a cobble on a cobbled street.

The next day, when I was taken before the jury, I remembered the set of the old film. It seemed to me that with the exception of Brett, every other protagonist in the scene had come straight from central casting, and a voice in the blackness beyond would shout out, "Cut!"

I watched the curious ritual with supreme detachment; as if I were not the hero of the piece, but a mere extra, as anonymous as a speck of caviar in its tin. The judge, a big, rotund man with yellowing sideburns, explained the circumstances of the drama to an abashed-looking group of upstanding citizens.

Marjorie was called. When she entered the room, I felt such acute emotion I thought I would faint. She was more beautiful than ever. I admired her modest demeanour and tact. She did not play the grief-stricken widow, was not dressed in premature mourning and wore her usual make-up. A young Englishwoman whose dignity commanded respect! Her reddened cheeks were the only hint that she might have been crying a great deal. She had mastered great sorrow, with tremendous courage, and I read the admiration that little bitch inspired in the tense faces all around.

In a neutral voice, devoid of passion or hatred, she explained how we had met in France, and how I had harassed her from that moment on. Listening to her, so calm and self-assured, I began to doubt my own story. Marjorie looked me in the eye, and I read nothing in her tranquil gaze but sorrow and pity. She gave the court to understand that I was an obsessive sex maniac. She had told me she was leaving for Scotland in an effort to shake me off, and she regretted it bitterly now that I had killed her husband and shattered her life! She had been dumbstruck at the sight of me when I appeared at Mrs Morton's bed and breakfast.

"At that moment," the dear soul declared, "I felt a dark premonition. I told my husband about the situation so that he wouldn't be surprised by the actions of Mr, er, I'm so sorry, but I don't remember his name."

Next, in her small but firm voice, she explained that on the day of the murder, I had followed her to the open-air theatre. I had sat next to her, assailing her with more passionate declarations. She had been forced to move away. The old, kilted gentleman who had sat beside me in the row of seats came to testify.

At 10 p.m., still according to Marjorie, I had called her husband at Mrs Morton's. I said I wanted to see him urgently. He had been reluctant to agree to a nocturnal meeting, and I had told him to think about it and call me back, at my hotel. This was what Nevil Faulks had decided to do, after half an hour's thought, despite the pleadings of his wife, who was terrified at the prospect of such a meeting. The whole story was a masterly construction. I listened, knowing full well that it was completely false, and marvelling at her skill in piecing it all together. Mrs Morton duly appeared, in a fine red coat with a fur collar, to confirm everything her lodger had said. She was plastered in war paint, and looked for all the world like the elderly, eccentric heroine of Giraudoux's play *The Madwoman of Chaillot*. After her, Inspector Brett took his place at the witness stand. He gave a thorough, succinct summary of his investigations, supported by readings from my statements. After that, the judge asked if I had anything to say.

And so I repeated my version of events, because it was the truth and I could say nothing but the truth as I knew it. But I could see that no one believed me. I adopted a measured tone, and strove to convince, but the looks I encountered registered nothing but incredulity or suspicion. As expected, the jury declared me guilty of the murder of Nevil Faulks, with malice aforethought, and I was informed that I would be brought before the next session of the Court of Justice in Edinburgh, for trial and sentencing.

With malice aforethought. That meant I would hang. My trial would serve only to confirm my sentence.

As I was leaving the courtroom, crossing a dark, panelled antechamber between my two guards, I saw Brett framed in a window. He was smoking his black pipe, and sniffing. His face was pale, and his cherry-red nose twitched like a rabbit's. I saw no one with him, and felt he was waiting for me. And indeed, he turned as I passed. I stopped abruptly, like a rearing horse. My guards were surprised, and hurried to clutch my arms.

"I have something to say to you, Inspector."

A flicker of interest lit his eyes, and he approached our group.

"Mr Brett," I said, "I suppose your work is finished. But I beg you to continue your investigation. I'm ready to sign a statement declaring myself guilty of murder with malice aforethought, if that will put your mind at ease, but before I pay the price, I want to know how Faulks's wife went about proving that I killed him at eleven o'clock at night, when I killed him at five o'clock in the afternoon! You're an honest police officer, Mr Brett, I'm sure of it. I'm counting on you!"

We stared at one another for a moment. He went on smoking his pipe, saying nothing. I felt an immense sorrow welling in my eyes. Tears poured down my cheeks; I couldn't wipe them away because my guards were still holding my arms.

"I killed him at five o'clock, Inspector. Five o'clock! You have to believe me!"

A man weeping is always a discomfiting sight, especially for a British gentleman like Brett. He wrinkled his small, pink rabbit's nose and turned his back on me, without a word.

I was no longer in police headquarters, but a proper prison, and my cell was a proper cell, as tradition dictated.

When a dog is about to die, he curls into a ball at the back of his kennel and rests his head on his paws, to await his end. I lay flat out on my bed, face downwards, and waited for mine. A strange calm came over me. Marjorie and her evil plans, the Scottish judges and their sentences faded into the background. I was alone with my conscience, with my crime. I had acted with malice aforethought all right. Oh! not days in advance, of course, but a good few seconds beforehand. And surely that came to the same thing? I could still feel the revolver in my hand. I saw Faulks's vile grin. I had killed him out of hatred. And Marjorie's scream of distress had done nothing to dissuade me.

I had always been a murderer. Because the thing we are driven to become in the space of three seconds is surely the thing we have always been, our innermost nature since birth.

"Well, then," I sighed, "let them hang me and be done!"

The following morning, I was in a deep sleep when a guard came to fetch me. He advised me to clean myself up, which surprised me somewhat. I entered the prison governor's office freshly shaven. Brett was there, flanked by two of his men. At the sight of him, I was unable to suppress a cheery wave of the hand.

"Something new, is there, Inspector?"

He looked surlier than ever. His forehead was marked with a purplish halo left by the leather lining in the rim of his felt hat. He wore a light-coloured suit. Instinctively, I turned to look out of the window. It was a fine day.

"You're going to come with us, to check a small detail," was his only response.

One of the men approached me with a set of handcuffs, but Brett stopped him with a raised arm. Hastily, I slipped my hands into my pockets.

In the prison yard, we climbed into an old black taxi. One of the inspectors took the wheel. Brett sat next to me, while his second colleague took one of the extra folding seats. As he did so, I noticed for the first time that he was wearing a white coat under his jacket.

"Where are we going?"

"You'll see!"

He sniffed harder than before. He must have shaved in a hurry: tufts of hair remained here and there on his chin. The taxi drove swiftly. There were few people about as yet. I recognized the crossroads and monuments. Edinburgh had imprinted itself on my mind, and I felt I had been living there for years. We drove down a steep street, bordered on one side by the rolling contours of Princes Street Gardens. "There'll be a reconstruction," I told myself. And the prospect alarmed me, because I felt unable to act out such an appalling scene. The more so because it would have no value as evidence, in the absence of Marjorie.

Quite unexpectedly, we did not stop in front of the gardens, but continued along the road. The taxi drove along Princes Street for a moment, then turned sharp right to follow the complicated twists and turns of a square marked out with bollards to direct the traffic. Finally, we pulled into a broad, short, quiet street lined with grey houses. The driver stopped between two front doors, beside a set of black railings. The behaviour of the police officers was impossible to fathom. The man sitting on the folding seat got out first and disappeared into the nearest house. We waited. The cop at the wheel lit a cigarette. Brett toyed with the big, velvet-covered armrest.

"And now?" I asked, pleadingly.

My companion shrugged his shoulders.

"Why won't you speak to me, Inspector? Don't you think my nerves have suffered enough?"

"I have nothing to say to you, Mr Valaise."

He stared insistently at the steps up which his white-coated colleague had climbed. I did the same, and a full fifteen minutes went by. Would I never stop waiting in this godforsaken city! With the noose around my neck, would they make me wait before the trapdoor fell away beneath my feet?

The second cop appeared at the top of the steps. But he was not alone. He was accompanied by a man. A tall, brown-haired man with a pale complexion. When I saw him, the world stopped turning for what seemed an eternity. My mouth had fallen wide open, but I was incapable of speech. I tried to stretch out a hand, but my arm felt like lead.

"Something the matter, Mr Valaise?" asked Brett, in that calm voice of his, shot through now with a hint of irony.

"That man! The man!" I croaked.

"What of him?"

"That's Nevil Faulks!"

22

My feelings were beyond comprehension. There were no words to express my incredulity, my state of shock, and my hopefulness. I feared I was mistaken, and wondered again if I had gone mad. I was desperate to get a closer look. Brett held me back as I made to dive out of the car door.

"Calm yourself."

His gruff voice held a note of unaccustomed warmth.

"Your reaction is not entirely unexpected," he added.

In a flash, I saw again the scene of the murder. Faulks's fierce, ironic sneer as he brandished the revolver. Our brief struggle, and Marjorie choking. And then the bullet I had fired quite deliberately into his head. Immediately, his skull had become a monstrous, blood-soaked thing. He had fallen face down in the grass, dead! Utterly dead! And the next morning, he was stiff in the falling rain and the dried blood covered his neck like a hideous coating of purplish-red plaster. No, the man walking slowly down the street with his back to me now couldn't be Nevil Faulks. This might be his twin brother, or his ghost… But it could not be the man I had killed and buried in the dark soil in the middle of the lawn.

"Let's go after them," I pleaded, "I want to get a closer look."

"You'll see him soon enough, Mr Valaise. My deputy is escorting him to my office. You'll get a good, long look at him there. But I'll have had a word with him beforehand…."

"That's not Nevil Faulks, is it?"

"Indeed. That man is not Nevil Faulks."

"His brother?"

"Nor his brother. That man's name is William Brent."

"The resemblance is astonishing."

"I think not."

"I swear, they're utterly alike!"

"And I swear that they are not. Both are tall and thin, but that's all. Brent doesn't even have brown hair, as Faulks did."

I stared at the two men walking away.

"On the contrary, just look! That man has brown hair!"

"His hair is dyed."

Brett pulled out a wad of papers he had been keeping stuffed inside his jacket, distorting its shape. There were newspaper cuttings, typed circulars, letters and photographs. Brett took one of the photographs and handed it to me. A portrait of an ascetic-looking man with charcoal eyebrows and a huge, prominent Adam's apple.

"Allow me to introduce you to Nevil Faulks, Mr Valaise."

I shook my head.

"No, Inspector, you're mistaken. I've never seen that man before."

"Oh, but you have! On that morning, when, looking out for Marjorie Faulks, you saw her on her husband's arm, on the other side of the street. You told me she had crossed the road to get close to you. You had eyes for her alone. Her companion was a mere silhouette. You didn't want to attract his attention. We never look too closely at a person we do not wish to look closely at us."

"But I saw him again that afternoon at the open-air theatre. And we stared straight at one another!"

"That was not Nevil Faulks, but the other man, Mr Valaise."

He tapped the window with his ring finger. It was the first time I had noticed his wedding ring. Until then, it hadn't once occurred to me that Brett might be married. The man was a machine sent to confuse me, a functionary charged with dispatching me to the scaffold as quickly as possible. The gold ring conjured a domestic existence in my imagination: an apartment, a wife, children, objects, smells... He lived somewhere in this city of blackened stone. Perhaps we had passed in front of his house?

The fake taxi was moving again. We sped past Brett's deputy and the man Brent, just as they were preparing to cross the road. The two men were talking, and Brent didn't see my astonished face pressed to the back window of the car.

"Where are they going?" I stuttered.

I feared the man would disappear into thin air, like the witches of ancient legend. Scotland is a land of ghosts, a place for magic of every kind.

"They're going to the police, but Brent thinks he's going to hospital."

"How so?"

"My deputy is posing as a nurse. He's telling Brent that Mrs Faulks has been the victim of a traffic accident, and is asking for him."

"But why the lie?"

"So that we can be sure this man knows Mrs Faulks. Clearly, he does know her, because he has gone along with Lawrence. I'm rather pleased with my little ruse."

Brett allowed himself a moment of self-congratulation. He stretched his legs on the folded-down seat opposite, crossed his hands on his stomach and breathed a long sigh through his sniffling nose.

"Lovely day, wouldn't you agree, Mr Valaise? Oh! While I think of it, I've a letter for you. Hmmm... let me see."

He gave a high-pitched whine as he searched through his poor, overstuffed pockets.

He pulled out a letter, folded in half. It came from France and I recognized the elegant hand immediately. It was from Denise.

"This came for you yesterday evening, at the Learmonth Hotel, and I took the liberty of opening it. You may not like its contents, Mr Valaise, but it has very probably saved your life."

I read:

> My poor, dear chump,
>
> Was Ivanhoe the First a cuckold? We shall never know. But Ivanhoe the Second certainly is. It happened the day after you left. Who? Narcissus, the blond beauty from the beach. His skin is like silk and he plays volleyball like a champion, but in bed, as elsewhere, he thinks only of himself. No, the only satisfaction I obtained from this magnificent numbskull was moral, not physical. He actually asked after you (not out of concern, but for fear you might return at any moment). I told him about your romantic idyll in the arms of Albion, and can you imagine the words that came of this angel's mouth? "I hope it wasn't the same one who tried to pull the car trick on me." I questioned him. No mistake, it was your own dearly beloved! To get into conversation with her chosen man without

losing face she pretends to get into the wrong car! It's really quite clever! But it didn't work on Narcissus – she wasn't his type. She left her beach bag in his car too, but Narcissus spotted it in time. Unlike you. In short, if you've been taken for the king of fools, I shouldn't be even half surprised.

You may think I'm being thoroughly nasty. It's true, I am. But there it is, there's only one thing more fragile than a woman's virtue, and that's her pride.

A loving word to end, all the same: missing you.

Je te…

Denise

I folded the letter. I felt bitter, and half dead with shame.

"This letter has proved the keystone of my investigation, Mr Valaise. When I read it, I suddenly understood that you were not lying, and that you were more victim than murderer. Nothing like a revelation of that order to set a policeman's mind ablaze!"

I said nothing, and he turned to look at me. I must have been wearing a curious expression indeed, because he began sniffing again in his corner of the car, staring out at the great herd of buses.

"If you've been taken for the king of fools, I shouldn't be even half surprised."

What was better? To be a murderer or a gullible fool? Perhaps I felt the loss of my status as a twisted murderer as failure of a kind? Brett would despise me more as a victim than as the guilty party. The king of fools! Was Ivanhoe the First a cuckold? I felt like a bystander on the margins of society, in the fog-bound limbo reserved for the shivering herd of my pathetic kind. Disaffected idealists! Ridiculed heroes! Scorned lovers!

My one moment of heroism had come the previous day, when the jury had declared me guilty of murder with malice aforethought.

"How did you do it, Mr Brett?"

He was daydreaming on his side of the car, and took a few moments to rouse himself.

"Do what, Mr Valaise?"

"Find out the truth?"

"I went through every statement in the folder with meticulous care: yours, and those of the witnesses."

"And so?"

"And so, one detail caught my attention. Mrs Faulks and Mrs Morton both assured me that you had called Nevil Faulks on the telephone, because he called you back. I went to your hotel and the manager, who also operated the switchboard, was positive. You hadn't called anybody. But he couldn't be certain that you had spent all evening in your room. He was down in the television room, and he thought you might have gone out again between nine and ten thirty. And so I concentrated on the second telephone call: the one Nevil had made to confirm your meeting. In the bed and breakfast, Mrs Morton makes outside calls at her guests' request, then connects them to their rooms. Her memory is poor, so she jots the numbers on a blackboard. The board is covered with numbers. *But none corresponds to the telephone number of the Fort William Hotel. And yet you took Faulks's call at the Fort William!"*

I was genuinely impressed.

"You are a fine detective, Mr Brett."

"Thank you."

"And what did you do next, if you don't mind my asking?"

"My men applied themselves to the task of checking every telephone number on Mrs Morton's board. Eventually, we found one that interested us. A furnished studio apartment, rented the day before the Faulkses arrived in Edinburgh, to a certain Mr Brent, from London. I decided to find out what the gentlemen in question looked like. I lay in wait, and he arrived..."

Brett was unable to resist... He removed his pipe from his pocket and began to fill it hurriedly. He hastened to take a couple of puffs before reaching police headquarters.

"And after that, Inspector?"

"When Brent arrived at the wheel of a pale-coloured MG, I felt I was on the right track. And so I allowed myself a small indiscretion. Once he was indoors, I searched the MG, though I had no warrant. In it, I found, how shall I put this... the key to the mystery! I'll show you just now, in my office."

"Come in, Mrs Faulks! I do apologize for this hasty call-out."

She entered the office with her habitual, light step. She was wearing black this time, and had applied no make-up. Her freckles looked like splashes of acid on her skin. When she saw me, she frowned slightly, then turned her head to indicate her clear intention to ignore me henceforward.

Brett showed himself eager, and attentive.

"Take this seat. I hope you didn't have any urgent business this morning?"

"I was returning to London!"

"With the transport strike still on..."

"In the hearse," she retorted, drily.

"Oh! I do beg your pardon, Mrs Faulks. Of course! Whatever was I thinking?"

Then, seating himself opposite her in the corner of the office, Brett looked her in the eye and said, very quietly:

"I thought you were planning to leave in Mr Brent's MG."

Marjorie's complexion turned an evil, earthy shade. Two dark circles had appeared under her eyes, and it seemed to me that her face had grown longer.

A faint buzzing was heard: Brett's tape recorder. It sounded like sweet music to me now.

"I have no idea what you're talking about, Inspector."

Brett opened a desk drawer and took out an object wrapped in white fabric. He pulled the fabric aside to reveal a revolver. One I thought I recognized.

"I'm talking about the man who owns this odd-looking weapon."

He pressed a button on his intercom.

"Come in for a moment, Morrow, and bring a white coat."

A few minutes passed. Brett swung his leg, and sniffed. Marjorie, her features a blur of anxiety, stared at the revolver and seemed to be having difficulty breathing. As for me, I felt I was watching some occult ritual whose proceedings were a complete mystery.

Morrow, the French translator with the appalling squint, came into the room. He had put on a white coat that was several sizes too big. Its front panels flapped about his ankles.

"Hello, Morrow!" Brett greeted him in jocular tones. He was in mischievous mood now. "Have you ever been shot at point-blank range?"

Morrow recoiled in mock horror.

"A bullet to the heart, my dear fellow! Here you go!"

Brett pointed the gun at Morrow's chest and pressed the trigger. A loud shot made the objects on Brett's desk shudder. A thin puff of smoke snaked around the room, floating on the air. I stared at Morrow's white coat, dumbfounded. For a moment, I thought Brett had killed his colleague. A large red stain was spreading over the cross-eyed man's chest.

"The powder's singed the coat a little, sir," Morrow observed, phlegmatically.

"Order another and charge it to the case!" said Brett.

And, turning to me:

"No expense spared. Whoever said we Scots were mean folk, eh, Mr Valaise?"

"That's the weapon I fired the other day, on the lawn, isn't it?"

"It is. The only thing it fires are haemoglobin capsules. But the illusion is perfect. Mrs Faulks led you away quickly, leaving you no time to discover the trick. Brent got up and cleaned himself off; he must have brought what he needed along with him. That evening, you were lured out of your hotel so that you had no alibi. It was Brent who called you. Certain that you were out and about in the deserted city, he met with poor Faulks, who was waiting for him, and led him to the deserted lawn. I have no idea under what pretext. This time, he fired a real bullet at the man's head, and it was a mask of real blood coating Faulks's scalp when you found him there the following morning."

"If you've been taken for the king of fools…"

Marjorie knew all was lost. She stood frozen, impassive, inhuman, staring out of the window at a world from which she was banished for ever.

"Your performance was beyond all expectations, Mr Valaise! These people allotted you a role, and your played it with rare gusto! Brent is your lover, naturally, Mrs Faulks?"

She made no reply.

"And you wanted rid of your husband. The crime was very cleverly constructed. A brilliant idea, to secure the collaboration of an innocent man from far away, unfamiliar with the country in which the murder would take place."

The word "innocent" had a pejorative sound in Brett's mouth. Or I was imagining things? The king of fools reads insinuations into everything.

Brett went to the door leading to the corridor and called out in loud, triumphant tones:

"Do come in now, Mr Brent."

Before Brent entered the room, I moved close to Marjorie, took her chin in my hand, and gazed ardently into her face.

"What if I hadn't fired?" I stammered. "Eh, Marjorie? If I hadn't fired, you would have failed completely?"

She gave a small, enigmatic smile.

"If you hadn't fired, Jean-Marie, then I would have done it myself. Me! Came to the same thing, didn't it? You're a brave man."

I must have blushed. I whispered a timid "Thank you" because her words comforted me a little.

Brent entered the office. He knew exactly what was afoot now, and gave a nod of defeat when he saw us.

"Take a seat, Mr Brent. You wrote the letter that was sent to Mr Valaise, did you not?"

Only a policeman would begin questioning a man accused of murder with something so seemingly unimportant.

Brent concurred, drily.

"I must warn you that whatever you say from now on will—"

"I know, Inspector."

"And it was also you who wrote the note that Mrs Faulks dropped on the pavement?"

"Naturally."

"How did Mrs Faulks come to have it in her hand at that moment?"

"She was going to leave it at the Learmonth. When she saw Mr Valaise, she decided to pass it to him in that way instead."

"And what if I had taken a good look at her husband just then?" I objected.

Brent turned to look at me.

"Marjorie would have told you later that I wasn't her husband, just a friend."

Marjorie! He pronounced her name in extraordinary, adoring tones, leaving no one in any doubt that he loved her, and would love her madly till the end of their adventure.

I felt a pang of envy.

"What did you tell Faulks, to get him out at such a late hour?"

"I knew about his business affairs, from Marjorie. I called him on behalf of one of his clients, who was due to leave on a cruise the following morning. I said there had been a last-minute decision… He was in bed and almost didn't come."

"I urged him to get up and go. And that was when he called Willy back, to tell him an agreement had been reached."

We were getting to the murder, the real murder. I felt a sudden reluctance to witness the rest of the interview.

"May I leave the room, Inspector? I have no business here now."

Brett stared at me in surprise, but I believe he understood.

"Could I see Nevil Faulks's body?" I asked.

The request seemed incongruous, yet there was a perfectly logical explanation for it.

"That's not possible for the moment," said Brett, "but you should know that Brent and Faulks were wearing the same suit. It's hardly surprising that you noticed nothing untoward on the lawn the next day, given the circumstances."

"May I step outside?"

"From the room, not the building. You are still guilty of concealing a body, Mr Valaise. I'm not able to free you here."

23

But the jury did, the next day.

When the king of fools becomes entangled in a plot of such complexity, pity and sympathy for his plight are the natural response.

With my acquittal came the end of the transport strike, and it was Brett himself who arranged for my seat on the plane.

In short, after a two-hour flight, I was back in Juan-les-Pins. It was 10 a.m., and Denise was already on the beach.

She was alone under our parasol. In just a few days, her skin had turned as dark as a prune.

She recognized my shadow before spotting me in the flesh, and quickly looked up.

"*Tiens!* Ivanhoe returns!" she sighed.

I dropped onto the burning sand beside her.

I gazed around, looking for the volleyball players, but the net hadn't been stretched into place.

"Are you looking for Narcissus?"

"Yes."

"He's not here yet. But don't bother about him. I was making it up. There was nothing between us."

"You're just saying that to—"

"I'm saying that because it's true. I wrote the letter in a fit of rage. When a girl discovers she's hitched herself to an utter creep for life, she's allowed the occasional tantrum, surely?"

"But what you said about Marjorie and the car..."

"All fibs! Anyway, it must have been fairly inspired stuff, because you came back. Admit it, without that telling detail, you would have stayed right there."

"You're right, that detail did the trick."

I gave a great, ferocious laugh. A laugh to devour the whole world. Denise's act of revenge had saved my life.

"Why are you laughing?"

"Because I'm happy!"

"Tell me…"

"What, my love?"

"If… if it had been true, Narcissus and me, what would you have done?"

"I don't know."

"Would you have killed him?"

"Perhaps…"

"Truly? You wouldn't dare."

My laughter died. I pulled myself up under the parasol until my head was inside the dark circle of shade. And it was a short while before I replied, gruffly:

"Oh, but I would!"

—

Did you know?

One of France's most prolific and popular post-war writers, Frédéric Dard wrote no fewer than 284 thrillers over his career, selling more than 200 million copies in France alone. The actual number of titles he authored is under dispute, as he wrote under at least 17 different aliases (including the wonderful Cornel Milk and l'Ange Noir).

Dard's most famous creation was San-Antonio, a James Bond-esque French secret agent, whose enormously popular adventures appeared under the San-Antonio pen name between 1949 and 2001. The thriller in your hands, however, is one of Dard's "novels of the night" – a run of stand-alone, dark psychological thrillers written by Dard in his prime, and considered by many to be his best work.

Dard was greatly influenced by the renowned Georges Simenon. A mutual respect developed between the two, and eventually Simenon agreed to let Dard adapt one of his books for the stage in 1950. Dard was also a famous inventor of words – in fact, he dreamt up so many words and phrases in his lifetime that a special dictionary was recently published to list them all.

Dard's life was punctuated by drama; he attempted to hang himself when his first marriage ended, and in 1983 his daughter was kidnapped and held prisoner for 55 hours before being ransomed back to him for 2 million francs. He admitted afterwards that the experience traumatised him for ever, but he nonetheless used it as material for one of his later novels. This was typical of Dard, who drew heavily on his own life to fuel his extraordinary output of three to five novels every year. In fact, when contemplating his own death, Dard said his one regret was that he would not be able to write about it.

AVAILABLE AND COMING SOON FROM PUSHKIN VERTIGO

Jonathan Ames

You Were Never Really Here

Augusto De Angelis

The Murdered Banker
The Mystery of the Three Orchids
The Hotel of the Three Roses

María Angélica Bosco

Death Going Down

Piero Chiara

The Disappearance of Signora Giulia

Frédéric Dard

Bird in a Cage
The Wicked Go to Hell
Crush
The Executioner Weeps
The King of Fools
The Gravediggers' Bread

Friedrich Dürrenmatt

The Pledge
The Execution of Justice
Suspicion
The Judge and His Hangman

Martin Holmén

Clinch
Down for the Count

Alexander Lernet-Holenia

I Was Jack Mortimer

Boileau-Narcejac

Vertigo
She Who Was No More

Leo Perutz

Master of the Day of Judgment
Little Apple
St Peter's Snow

Soji Shimada

The Tokyo Zodiac Murders
Murder in the Crooked Mansion

Masako Togawa

The Master Key
The Lady Killer

Emma Vickic

Resurrection Bay

Seishi Yokomizo

The Inugami Clan

ALSO AVAILABLE FROM PUSHKIN VERTIGO

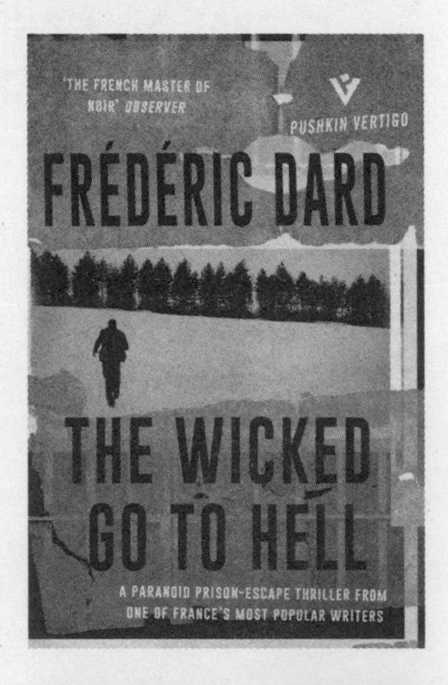

Find out more at **www.pushkinpress.com**